January 2021

Mathew Klickstein
illustrated by Michael S. Bracco

The Kids of

WIDNEY JUNIOR HIGH

Take Over the World!

Schiffer Kids™

4880 Lower Valley Road, Atglen, PA 19310

Library of Congress Control Number: 2020930457

Designed by Brenda McCallum
Type set in Archer

ISBN: 978-0-7643-6018-3
Printed in The United States of America

Published by Schiffer Kids
An imprint of Schiffer Publishing, Ltd.
4880 Lower Valley Road
Atglen, PA 19310
Phone: (610) 593-1777; Fax: (610) 593-2002
E-mail: Info@schifferbooks.com
Web: www.schifferbooks.com

For our complete selection of fine books on this and related subjects, please visit our website at www.schifferbooks.com. You may also write for a free catalog.

Schiffer Publishing's titles are available at special discounts for bulk purchases for sales promotions or premiums. Special editions, including personalized covers, corporate imprints, and excerpts, can be created in large quantities for special needs. For more information, contact the publisher.

We are always looking for people to write books on new and related subjects. If you have an idea for a book, please contact us at proposals@schifferbooks.com.

> "After I learn the bass,
> I'm going to take over the world!"

Cain, KOWJH Member

THE KIDS OF WIDNEY HIGH is a raucous rock band composed of members living with various disabilities who sing about their hopes, fears, and dreams ... also cows, insects, and the joy of getting a new car.

Having blossomed out of a music class based out of special-education school Joseph P. Widney High, the group is led by former teacher Michael Monagan. Among other adventures along the way of producing four full-length albums and playing shows throughout the greater Los Angeles area, the Kids were prominently featured in the hit Farrelly Brothers–produced comedy *The Ringer,* starring Johnny Knoxville and Katherine Heigl.

For more on the Kids, please visit:
www.KidsOfWidneyHigh.com

Although what follows is a work of fiction, we gratefully acknowledge the band for allowing us to be inspired by their unique spirit and for their encouraging support throughout the completion of this book.

We are delighted to give a portion of the profits from this book to L.A. GOAL (Greater Opportunities for Advanced Living), a nonprofit in the Los Angeles area that has been offering recreational, artistic, and employment opportunities to persons with disabilities for the past five decades. Their program and clients greatly inspired 2001's *I Am Sam*, for which the film's star, Sean Penn, received an Oscar nomination. Artwork made by clients of L.A. GOAL was used for the Kids of Widney High's third album, *Act Your Age*, and the organization remains a supportive partner and friend of the band. www.LAGOAL.org

CHAPTER 1

The New Kid Is Not So New

Here are two things that might go through your head if you ever get shoved up against a locker during your first week of sixth grade:

(1) *Huh! This kind of thing actually happens?*

(2) *Exactly what brand of garbage does this dragon-breath monster twice my size holding me up by the neck eat for breakfast?*

You may also wonder (along with how hard he can squeeze that scrawny neck of yours before your head pops like a grape): *Gosh, how did I get here?*

Or maybe you're one of those people who never has to worry about getting shoved up against a locker (or pantsed or tripped or forced to go out in the rain and sing the National Anthem backward three times in a row).

Well, it only took me a few days at Widney before I became one of those people who *does* get shoved up against a locker.

Or at least I *was* one of those people until I met the Kids of Widney Junior High and watched them on their way to becoming one of the greatest rock bands of all time—which is what my story is all about. (You probably already guessed this: Heck, it's the title of this book!)

Now, *you* may never have heard of the Kids of Widney Junior High before. But I first got to know them because I go to Widney Junior High School, where the Kids are in the special-education program.

Me, I'm just in the boring, garden-variety classes with the rest of the boring, garden-variety students.

Not that there's anything necessarily wrong with being boring and garden-variety. It's just that the Kids of Widney Junior High really *are* something special. Take Peewee, for instance. In addition to his autism, he lives with legal blindness. Yet, that guy still sees a whole lot more than you'd think. (Just keep him away from your cat. Or too much toilet paper. More on that kind of thing later.)

So Widney has sixth-, seventh-, and eighth-graders. Being in sixth grade, I'm one of the younger kids. I'm eleven. Some of the older kids can get up there: we're talking *thirteen!!*

If you ask me, having the older kids with the younger kids is a little weird. Since no one *did* ask me, I guess we've got no choice in the matter. If things *were* up to me, I'd make it so we could watch more movies in school. And, you know, *good* ones.

But that's something else again.

My parents and I moved around a bunch before I got to Widney. This means I had to get good at meeting new people quickly. Tips for those who are curious include:

(1) Mashing your food together at the lunch tables and eating it, no matter how disgusting it might be. (Careful with grape juice and nacho cheese. You'd *think* that combination would go down easier than it does, but nope. It doesn't.)

(2) Writing funny little sayings on the chalkboard behind the teacher's back without her knowing it, on your way into and out of the classroom. (I find the best stuff in old books from the 1920s. The Marx Bros., *Krazy Kat* comic strips, old *Popeye* cartoons . . .)

(3) Always make sure to shower. Being the "new kid" is *way* easier than being the "stinky kid."

Usually these kinds of things made me comfortably popular early on at my new schools . . . even though they also just as easily landed me in detention.

At Widney, though, something was different.

The old tricks to make friends didn't seem to work anymore. Maybe it was because sixth-graders and everyone older care more about what kinds of clothes you wear or what music you listen to than about how many gummy bears and mashed potatoes you can shove into your mouth at once.

But, like Peewee would later tell me, I don't want to tell you "no sob stories."

Which reminds me—I should probably give you my name since I *am* the one telling this tale.

I'm Robbie Wilson (I know: boring, garden-variety name. But that's yet *another* thing no one bothered asking me about before it happened). I'm an only child (which I highly recommend during the gift-getting holidays, though not so much when something gets broken around the house and you have no one else to blame).

I'm not big into sports (I'm kinda small), but I *do* watch a *lot* of movies. I also read a *ton*—which started confusing my mom. It was pretty funny to watch as Mom realized she couldn't really punish me by taking away my TV privileges, because I'd just go upstairs and read instead.

That may seem weird to some of you out there, but you don't know *anything* about weird until you meet the Kids of Widney Junior High.

CHAPTER 2

Peewee and the Great Peanut Butter and Jelly Sandwich Fight

It was maybe the fourth or fifth day of school and I was walking down the hallway at Widney. Not the easiest thing to do with so many people bumping into you from every direction. Rather than whining about it, though, I simply kept my head down.

Which turned out to be a *big* mistake.

I bumped right into a group of guys twice my size. And they didn't appear to be very happy about that. One of them had a mustache, I think. Or maybe that was chocolate smudged across his upper lip. Either way, *yikes*.

Here I was, the new kid at a school where no one seemed too interested in how fresh and clean I smelled from my many, many showers. Instead, I was about to get pummeled

by these ogres, who probably should have graduated already.

Did I mention one of them may have had a mustache?

"'Sup, dude?" the burly bear of a boy asked.

"Oh, man! My bad!" I said, thinking it would come out as cool.

I was mistaken. *Profoundly* mistaken.

I tried to push through as the bell rang, but that didn't work, either.

You'd think this would be one time when having so many people at the school would be a plus. But no one seemed bothered by the fact that this tiny kid was clearly about to be torn apart by five guys who probably got out of jail the day before.

"Oh, excuse me," I said, politely trying to get by the human mountain with the maybe-mustache once more.

"There's no excuse for *you*," he said, ramming me up against a locker.

"What kinda nonsense is this?" someone called out from down the hall.

We all turned to his voice. Since I was still pinned up against the locker with Mr. Maybe-Mustache and his friends blocking my view, I couldn't see who was approaching.

I could *hear* him, though: "You guys causing some trouble?"

The mystery man must have looked to my bullies like even more of a loser than I did, because they started laughing.

"Dude," one of the bullies chuckled. "It's a special-ed kid!"

They pointed and laughed even louder than before.

I finally saw the guy with the voice, and he was hardly taller than me. He was like this . . . this *mini-man* with a slight mustache of his own, brownish skin, and black hair buzzed short.

He also had THE *biggest* glasses I've ever seen. We're talking fishbowls. His eyes were *huge* behind those lenses! He was like a comic book character. Only, the kind *I* would have drawn. If I could draw.

"Leave that kid alone, ya *jabronis!*" the guy with giant glasses said. He was closing in and didn't seem afraid at all. (Probably thanks to his having a mustache of his own. A *real* one.)

"Jabronis?!" The bullies began laughing so hard that I thought they were going to explode.

No such luck.

Instead, Mr. Maybe-Mustache said to the guy with the giant glasses, "Get back to your special-ed class and make more cotton-ball snowmen or whatever you do in there!"

That was right when the bullies stopped laughing.

They probably saw what I saw.

I'm telling you, the glasses of this comic book character in front of me fogged up like someone had painted them over. He was *fuming.*

Then he did something *really* wild: he smirked.

Out of nowhere, Mr. Maybe-Mustache and his gigantic cohorts were being pelted with about fifteen peanut butter and jelly sandwiches.

BOOM! SPLAT! SPLURGE!

It all became slow motion, and the comic book character kept taking out more and more sandwiches from his backpack, chucking them at the bullies without stopping.

Two of the bullies fell backward onto the ground. Two others—including Mr. Maybe-Mustache—snatched a few sandwiches from the floor and threw them back at my strange protector, but that didn't seem to slow him down.

Everything was still in slow motion, as I bounded away from the battlefield, peanut butter and jelly sandwiches flying around me like fireworks.

BOOM! SPLAT! SPLURGE!

Even though it was this comic book character versus two other huge guys—with their friends cowering in balls on the ground, covered in sticky grape jelly and gooey peanut butter—he kept up the good fight.

BOOM! SPLAT! SPLURGE!

I watched, amazed. But before I could even try to figure out what in blazes was going on, we all heard over the loud speaker:

"PEEWEE TO THE PRINCIPAL'S OFFICE . . . IMMEDIATELY!"

The comic book guy in the fishbowl glasses hurled two last peanut butter and jelly sandwiches, whacking my bullies in the face. "Sorry, boys. They're playing my song!"

He dashed past me, his open backpack trailing peanut butter and jelly sandwiches behind him. I flattened myself up against the locker to stay out of his way as he zipped by, saying, "Meet me in the music room after school."

"Wait!" I called after him. "Who *are* you?"

"You heard the announcement!" he shouted over his shoulder as he ran. "Peewee!"

And with that, he was gone.

I was alone again. With these five monster men writhing in a moaning, groaning, sticky mess on the ground at my feet. Peanut butter and jelly was *everywhere*.

I looked up to the low ceiling, as a sandwich plopped down in front of me.

That was my first encounter with a member of the Kids of Widney Junior High.

CHAPTER 3

My First Rehearsal

I was too curious not to meet up with Peewee in the music room after school.

"What you did earlier today was absolutely *incredible!*" I couldn't help myself from blurting out when we met up.

"Eh," Peewee huffed as he led me out of Widney to the front parking lot. "I always keep plenty of peanut butter and jelly sandwiches in my backpack, just in case."

Who *was* this guy? (And why had he called those other dudes *jabronis?* Whatever those were.)

"What?" Peewee asked, seeing I was confused.

"Nothing," I said. "You talk kind of funny."

"Yeah? Well, you *looked* kind of funny right before those *jabronis* were gonna kick your butt."

Peewee and I shared a laugh over this, and he reached up to pat me on the shoulder. I felt this strange sense that he was acting like an older brother . . . if I had had one.

"Where're you taking me?" I asked.

"To practice. You gotta meet my band."

We ended up heading over to Mr. Monagan's house.

He's Widney's music teacher, and Peewee's band turned out to be a bunch of special-ed students Mr. Monagan teaches during fifth period.

We went through a door on the side of the house, and there we were in Mr. Monagan's garage.

I'd never been in a teacher's house before, but there were pictures of Mr. Monagan all over the walls, each showing him with some of my all-time favorite musicians. There was Mr. Monagan with They Might Be Giants, Mr. Monagan with Devo, and even Mr. Monagan with "Weird Al" Yankovic!

Turns out Widney's only music teacher used to be a real rocker back in the day. He gave it up in order to teach. Then he started the Kids of Widney Junior High.

"Ah, Peewee," Mr. Monagan said in a soft voice from behind his small glasses, mad-scientist gray hair, and large acoustic guitar. "Late as always."

"You talkin' stuff again, Michael?" Peewee said in what I was coming to find was his Peewee way.

I thought it was pretty wild that Peewee would call a teacher by his first name, even out of school. But then things got even wilder.

"Look at Tanesa!" Peewee said, pointing a stubby finger at an older girl with very dark skin and curly black hair resting her head on a nearby speaker. "She's not even awake!"

Grinning that knowing grin of his, Peewee then asked, "And where's everyone else?"

Mr. Monagan played a quick excerpt of a Beatles song (really, really well) before chuckling, "Well . . . Shelly's upstairs with my daughters watching *Titanic*. Again. Daniel's listening to the presidential debate on the radio in the kitchen. Cain and Elisa are still on their way with Elisa's dad driving. Which means they're probably lost . . ."

"Wait a second," I couldn't help but interrupt. "This is a *band?*"

"This," Mr. Monagan said, beaming proudly and playing another quick excerpt from a Beatles song, "is the Kids of Widney Junior High."

CHAPTER

Never Give Honey Nut Cheerios to Cain

It was maybe a half hour later that Elisa's dad finally dropped off Elisa and Cain at Mr. Monagan's house.

"Well, look who's here," Mr. Monagan said, finishing what I had learned a few minutes earlier was a "hot lick" on his guitar. "The Gruesome Twosome."

"Heh-hello . . . Mr. . . . Monagan," Cain said.

Cain and Elisa looked somewhat alike. Not like they were related, but something about them still struck me as similar. They kind of reminded me of the Oompa Loompas from *Willy Wonka & the Chocolate Factory*. The old one, not the new. (I *hate* the new one! Yikes!)

The only difference was they weren't orange. They were more of a caramel color, like Peewee. It was interesting getting to meet all these new people. And I had only been at Widney a few days!

(Oh, yeah, Elisa and Cain didn't have green hair like the Oompa Loompas, either. But they kind of waddled around like those lovable characters from one of my favorite films, and they were just as energetic and welcoming.)

Cain came right up to me and introduced himself, putting his hand out a bit to my left. "*Hola, ¿qué tal?*" Cain said. "M-my name is . . . Cain." (I think it's important to note here that you pronounce Cain like "Ky-een." *Not* like "Cain" from the story of Cain and Abel.)

"This is our new friend Robbie Wilson, Cain," Mr. Monagan called out, not getting up from his chair. He then played a few chords, as they turned out to be called, on his guitar. "Move your hand a *little* to your left, Cain. That's where Robbie's standing."

Aside from learning how to correctly pronounce Cain's name, I quickly discovered that whereas Peewee was *legally* blind, Cain was *completely* blind. One of his eyes had been removed when he was a baby, in fact. You couldn't tell, though, because he always kept his eyelids shut. He also *always* had a big, happy grin on his chubby face.

Yup, I liked Cain right away. Something about him made me feel like he was the nicest guy I'd ever met.

Cain moved his hand closer to me and we shook.

When I realized he was blind, I turned to ask Mr. Monagan if he was going to touch my face like I'd seen in the movies.

"Why don't you ask him yourself?" Mr. Monagan said, not looking up from his "fingering" and guitar.

"Oh," I suddenly realized aloud. "I'm sorry! Yeah, Cain, do you want to touch my face? That's . . . what, um . . . that's what blind people do, right?"

Peewee and Elisa laughed at this.

I turned and saw they were hugging each other and not letting go. Elisa, I'd later learn, was Peewee's girlfriend. And the story of how *they* got together is a really fun one I'd get to hear later. (Don't worry: I'll keep you in the loop on all that.)

But for now, I had to learn an important lesson about people who live with blindness.

"Hey, new kid," Elisa said, letting go of Peewee, who in turn let go of her to walk over to me. "If you're gonna hang out with the Kids of Widney Junior High, there are a few things we need to get straight first. Okay?"

Elisa wasn't being mean. In fact, she would end up being almost as nice a person as Cain and Peewee, I'd find. I'd also later find out that Elisa lives with some minor intellectual disability, like Tanesa and Cain. Meaning some things can be a little more difficult than others for her to understand, read, say, or do. But that never seemed to matter, because as I'd *also* find out, Elisa can do and does just about *everything!*

She's big on speaking her mind and sees herself as something of a leader of the group. Even though the group doesn't really have any leaders; they're a band: *All for one and one for all.* Just like the Three Musketeers! (Another favorite movie of mine; the old one, not the new one!)

"So," Elisa started, "blind people . . . we don't touch people's faces. That's something that only happens in movies or TV shows. You can't believe everything you see or read, right?"

"It's n-n-not t-t-true," Cain agreed.

"Yeah, that's all just some crazy talk!" Tanesa said from her chair, joining in on the conversation, watching over us all. (If *any* of the Kids of Widney Junior High was a "leader," it was Tanesa. Mainly because she was the oldest.)

"Oh, I'm sorry again," I said. I was worried I was making a bad impression. There I went, making mistake after mistake again. I'm probably the best mistake-maker around. It's my one true talent.

"It's okay," Cain said. "Can I . . . give you a hug . . . t-t-to m-make you f-f-feel better?"

I couldn't believe he wanted to give *me* a hug! After I had practically just insulted him, he wanted to make *me* feel better! I was relieved to know they all still thought I was okay. No one was yelling at me or telling me to leave. It was then I knew that even though I might not have known everything about them, and even though I was making some mistakes, I would be a welcome part of their group from then on.

It made me feel really good about myself. It wasn't often that I found a group of other people like that. People who weren't so judgmental; people who understood that it was okay to mess up.

I hugged Cain and he hugged me.

Then Elisa hugged us both.

Then Tanesa got up and hugged all three of us.

We were one big hug bug!

"All right, all right," Mr. Monagan said, not getting up from his chair as he put aside his guitar. "We're at rehearsal here, gang. Which means we need to play some music!"

The hug bug let go of one another, Elisa waddled back to Peewee, who had opted out of the group hug (which wasn't really his thing, he'd later explain), Tanesa went back to her chair, and Cain stood there waiting for whatever was next with his big Cain smile on his face.

He began rocking back and forth as though he was listening to some kind of rock music in his head. I liked the way Cain did that. He was in his own groove.

"Tanesa, could you please go get Shelly and Daniel from upstairs?" Mr. Monagan asked.

"I guess I gotta do *everything* around here, huh, Michael?"

Tanesa and Mr. Monagan shared a laugh about this, and I found it really weird again that some of the kids called Mr. Monagan Mr. Monagan and some of them—like Peewee and Tanesa—called him by his first name.

"Now, before we get started," Mr. Monagan said, exhaling deeply, "I want to know why you guys were so late. Is everything okay with your dad, Elisa?"

"Oh, yeah, Mr. Monagan," Elisa said, standing up out of her embrace from Peewee, who was sharing a large easy chair with her. "It wasn't my dad's fault this time. I swear."

"All right, all right," Mr. Monagan said. "I believe you. Just tell me what happened. We can't keep doing this every time. Everyone else has their own schedules we need to think about too, and whenever we're late like this, it affects us *all*."

"I know, I know," Elisa said, concerned. "But what it was was, see, we had to pick up Cain from his doctor's appointment, and when we did, they told us Cain still had a few more tests left, and that's why we had to take extra time and why we were late getting here."

"Ohhhh," Mr. Monagan said, slapping his forehead. "I completely forgot. Cain, did you have some tests for your sugar levels today?"

"Yes, I *doooo*," Cain said, rocking back and forth harder. "Yes, yes, m-m-m-y sugar levels. Yeah." I would come to learn that Cain has a unique way of speaking that isn't always *technically* correct but adds to his equally unique charm.

Mr. Monagan turned to me and explained that Cain has diabetes. He requires special shots of something called insulin in his stomach several times a day to make sure he stays healthy. Diabetes is *not* contagious, and it's not that uncommon.

Aside from the regular shots they need, people living with diabetes also have to be really careful about how much sugar they eat.

Diabetics can end up with some pretty serious problems—like passing out in a coma—if they have too much sugar. It's not good. Luckily, it's manageable if they're careful and go to the doctor to keep up with their tests.

"Wow," I said, "so you can't have any Kit-Kat bars or Reese's Peanut Butter Cups, Cain?"

"N-n-no. No sugar," Cain said, rocking back and forth so fast now I was impressed. He kept that smile on his face, so I knew he wasn't nervous as much as he was just doing his own Cain thing.

"He can have a *little* bit of sugar sometimes," Mr. Monagan said. "Just not *too* much."

"Remember that time at *camp*, Mr. Monagan?" Elisa asked.

"Ohhh!" Mr. Monagan chuckled, leaning his head back and closing his eyes. "We all went to this adaptive camp up in Big Bear a few years ago, and some of the special-ed counselors were giving out breakfast to everyone . . . "

"Uhhhh oh!" Peewee said. "I remember *that*. Oh, heck yeah! Cain ate all those Honey Nut Cheerios and everyone was *freaking OUT, dude!* Holy moly!"

I was shocked. "Wait a second; you're not supposed to eat sugar, and you had a whole bowl of Honey Nut Cheerios, Cain?"

"Honey Nut Cheerios, yeah!" Cain said.

"What happened?" I asked.

"He was fine," Elisa said. "But all the counselors were going absolutely crazy when they realized what had happened. It was totally scary."

"Nahhhhh," Peewee said. "It was funny as heck. I knew Cain'd be okay, right, Cain? You're a tough *hombre.*" Peewee patted Cain on the back, and for the first time since he'd started, Cain stopped rocking back and forth. He reached out and Peewee helped him put his arm around his neck.

Mr. Monagan explained that what had happened was that only one counselor at the camp knew about Cain's diabetes, and it was a different counselor who gave him the same breakfast—the sugary Honey Nut Cheerios—that the rest of the special-ed campers were eating. Once the counselor who knew better saw what was happening, she bolted over to pull the bowl away from Cain. But he eats so fast, most of it was already gone!

"Peewee's right," Mr. Monagan said, smiling down at Peewee and Cain together. "Cain's a tough cookie and he was just fine. A tiny amount of sugar is okay."

Cain smiled even bigger than before, and Peewee put his arm around Cain's neck too. They were obviously good friends.

This is a real band! I thought to myself. *Look how well they get along and know each other!*

I couldn't wait to hear their music.

I'd get my wish, because right then, Tanesa came down with Shelly and Daniel. The rehearsal was at long last about to start.

CHAPTER 5

Shelly Knows More About Movies Than Anyone You'll Ever Meet!

I think my favorite part about a Kids of Widney Junior High rehearsal is how laid back everyone is.

There's no stress. No pressure. It's easygoing and *fun*. Everyone cracks jokes and talks about what they've been up to over the week; how classes are going; whatever they might have coming up in the next week.

It's almost like the Kids are more of a club than a band.

They just happen to play really, really killer rock music that you can dance to. Cain and Shelly especially rock out whenever they play. It would be a while before I'd get to see my first full-on Kids of Widney Junior High concert. But during those rehearsals, *man*, Shelly and Cain can *get down!*

Daniel is the one member of the group who takes everything a bit too seriously. The Kids are really important for him, and I'd later learn that it's because he sees the group as a way to help people outside the disabled community understand said community in a better way.

Mainly the notion that not everyone in the disabled community is the same; some people with disabilities don't even like being lumped into that category at all. But, that's something that would come up more when I'd get to spend some time alone with Daniel later on.

Elisa does her best to remember her lyrics and have good posture during rehearsals. She can take the "job" of being in the band more seriously than some of the others. In that way she's closer to Daniel in sensibility about it all, I guess. But whereas Daniel is all into the band's "message," so to speak, Elisa is into doing a good job so the audience will have a great time. For her, the music itself is the thing.

Cain and Peewee are *all* about the fun. They're forever laughing and having a blast when they're singing. And because of that, they know the audience will have a fantastic time along with them.

Mr. Monagan, of course, is not only their teacher, but also their band leader. He does most of the instrumentation. During my first rehearsal, I got to see him really get into it with his acoustic guitar. But I'd later see him rock out *all the way* with his electric guitar on stage during my first concert to come.

Tanesa messes around with a tambourine, and she's usually the main one leading the group, like I said before.

She sometimes has some trouble with her movement due to having something called cerebral palsy. But it definitely doesn't stop her from rocking out at concerts and rehearsals!

Because Tanesa's the oldest, at thirteen and a half, the rest of the band watches and listens to her for the guidance they need to all be one cohesive group of singers.

That's the trick: the Kids of Widney Junior High are mostly a singing group, like something you'd see at church or synagogue, at camp or school choir. Or maybe on the Disney Channel. Sometimes they'll have different friends of Mr. Monagan's come to play drums or the bass or even harmonica. But Mr. Monagan does such an amazing job on his guitar, you don't really need any other instruments to play along with the group in order to get what they're all about.

When I was in the car with Shelly later, on the way home (since he lives close to me and his mom offered me a ride), he told me they all write the songs together in class. It's like a crowd-sourced kind of thing, which I think is totally cool.

They're all in it *together*.

Which reminds me! I forgot to talk about what Shelly is like when he's singing at rehearsal.

If Tanesa is like the leader, Shelly is probably best described as the spirit. He keeps the vibe up. And as I'd later see at their concerts, he's the one who calls out to the crowds and gets everyone all riled up, clapping and laughing and singing along and dancing with the band.

Shelly can't stop moving, hopping up and down, swinging around his arms and really showing what the Kids of Widney Junior High can do at full throttle. He's almost as old as Tanesa, and he's *really* tall. Like Peewee, Shelly is autistic. *Unlike* Peewee, he doesn't have a *mustache*. Though, that's only because Shelly shaves. Which is pretty wild for someone who's thirteen, but that's good ol' Shelly for you!

On the ride home, Shelly and his mom started talking with me about my favorite movies, since it came up that I can't get enough of 'em. Sure, I love watching movies. I love talking about movies. But I've never met anyone who loves watching and talking about movies as much as Shelly.

"Ask him a year," Shelly's mom said, driving and smiling in the reflection of the rearview mirror, which Shelly and I could see from the back seat.

"What do you mean?" I asked.

"Any year at all," Shelly's mom said again. "Ask him. You'll see."

"Uhhh . . . ," I stammered. "1937?"

"Shelly, what movie won Best Picture at the Academy Awards in 1937?" Shelly's mom asked into the rearview mirror.

"Best Picture 1937?" Shelly asked.

"Yeah, tell your new friend Robbie which movie won the Oscar."

"That would beeeee . . ." Shelly thought about it briefly before answering with a huge grin, "*The Great Ziegfeld.* Starring William Powell, Myrna Loy, and Luise Rainer."

"Wow!" I said, not exactly sure what a "ziegfield" was or

what might make one "great." I asked Shelly how he knew the winner, and he said he really *loves* movies. A lot.

"Shelly knows every Academy Award winner, Robbie," his mom said. "Shelly, who won for Best *Costume Design* in 1937?"

Shelly, still smiling bright and looking out the window shaking his head, said, "Noooo, Mom. There *wasn't* a Best Costume Design winner in 1937. Because . . . of course, yeah, the first award for *that* category wasn't given out untilllllllll . . . 1948."

"And who won that first year?" Shelly's mom and I asked at the same time, excited now to find out from our very own Academy Award Google search sitting right in the car with us.

"Yeaaahhhh, well, of course it went to *two* winners that first year, one for Roger K. Furse for *Hamlet* and one for Dorothy Jeakins and Barbara Karinska for *Joan of Arc*. Dorothy Jeeeeeeakins! Jeakins Jeakins Jeakins."

"That's incredible!" I said.

I guess the tidbit about *Hamlet* got Shelly thinking about Shakespeare, because then he began gleefully talking at length about the playwright behind such other great works as *Romeo and Juliet* and *Macbeth*. Shelly said that whenever people perform *Macbeth* today, which is really rare, they always call it "the Scottish Play" because of some kind of curse they all think is on the play. So they have to be *really* careful when performing it. So careful that, yeah, they won't even call it by its actual title!

I couldn't *believe* how many of these fascinating facts Shelly knew about Shakespeare and "the bard's" plays—and some of the buildings we passed by out the window too.

But what Shelly knows about *movies* takes the cake. For the rest of the car ride home, he would answer every single question I had about any movie—who made it, who starred in it, what year it came out . . .

Shelly's mom got into the game too and would ask him questions, and even if it was something as obscure as who won for Best Production Design in 1968 (John Box and Terence Marsh for *Oliver!*), Shelly would get it right.

I was a little disappointed when they pulled up to my house. But I couldn't wait to tell my mom about my new friend Shelly and his amazing talent for memorizing Academy Awards and movie trivia. And, oh yeah, of course my incredible afternoon spent with the Kids of Widney Junior High.

CHAPTER 6

A Day with Tanesa

RINNNNNNG!

RINNNNNNG!

"Mmmf," I said, still asleep.

RINNNNNNG!

"MMMMFFF!" I said again. Didn't anyone hear me? I *said* "Mmmmfff!"

Wait. *Who was I talking to?*

Answer: no one. Reason: it was early. *Too* early. Too early to have anyone over. Too early to be out of bed. Too early . . . for someone to be calling me on my cell phone!

I checked my phone. Yes, it was Saturday. A day I was *supposed* to be able to sleep in. A day when *everyone*, I thought, was supposed to be sleeping in.

Apparently not.

I checked the phone again. *Argh: 6:20. A! M!* And *who*, you're probably wondering, would dare call me so early? On a Saturday?

TANESA.

That's what my screen said.

I picked up.

"Robbie? It's Tanesa," I heard squawking out of the phone.

"Mmmmfff."

"Robbie, is that you? It's Tanesa from the Kids of Widney Junior High."

"Mmmmfff," I said again, in case she missed it the first time.

"Okay, so Robbie, I *think* it's you over there," Tanesa said. "I wanna know if you wanna come over today. If you're gonna be hangin' 'round with our band, I just wanna, you know, like get to know you better and stuff."

"Uhhh," I said, having run out of mmmmfffs. "Yeah, I mean . . . maybe in a few hours—"

"Nooo," Tanesa cut me off. "Uh uh. We gotta get together *now*. 'Cause, like, I got stuff to do later, and I wanna make sure we get a chance to meet up. The Kids are really important to me, Robbie, and I like to get to know and make sure anyone who's gonna be around now is, like, you know, a good perrrrson and has his heart in the right pllllllaaaaace and, you know, is fun to be 'round."

"I'm fun to be 'round," I said, waking up a little more. Tanesa was taking this whole thing almost as super-serious as Daniel, and I wanted her to know I was down for whatever she needed. Meeting the Kids was one of the best things that had happened to me in *months*. I didn't want to upset their leader, or whatever Tanesa was.

I couldn't imagine what we'd be up to. By the time I finally got myself out of bed (7:02 a.m.), finished showering (7:22 a.m.), made and ate breakfast (7:55 a.m.), and got my early-worm mom to drive me over to the address Tanesa had texted me (8:20 a.m.), I'd find out.

The door to Tanesa's house opened before I had a chance to knock, and out popped the Kids of Widney Junior High member herself, raring and ready to go. (Didn't she know it was only 8:20 in the morning? And did I mention it was a *SAT-UR-DAY?*)

"Okay, getcho stuff, and let's go, Robbie," Tanesa said, walking down her steps and away from me. I realized I was supposed to follow her, so I did. I gotta admit, when it comes to following, I'm one of the best followers around.

While I walked behind Tanesa, who seemed particularly driven (something I'd find out was one of her main characteristics), I couldn't help admiring her hairdo.

She was talking about how she got into the band, and how she's been with them for four years now, why she loves singing, and why she started playing the tambourine seven months, twenty-two days, and four hours ago.

I was looking at her hair.

The last time I'd seen Tanesa—when we were at Mr. Monagan's house earlier in the week—her hair was long and curly. This time, it was a big poof like a fluffy globe above her head.

Over the next few weeks, I'd see that Tanesa was the kind of person who likes to change her makeup, outfit, glasses, and hair *a lot*. Each time I'd see her, she'd look like a completely different person. It was a nifty trick.

"Hey, Tanesa?" I asked, and she stopped talking for a moment but continued walking. She didn't turn around when she asked, "Yeah, Robbie? Wussup?"

"How did you do that to your hair?" I asked timidly. I knew it might not be the most polite thing to simply come out and ask someone about her choice of appearance. But I was also curious. And I guess my curiosity won out in the end. Sometimes people like all my questions. Sometimes they don't. I hoped Tanesa was part of the first group.

"Oh," Tanesa said, still not turning around or stopping, "it's just something I be doin'. I like hair. It's so nice to play with it and make it look all gooood, donchu think?"

"I think it looks *great*, Tanesa!" I said, and I meant it.

Tanesa finally stopped and turned around. She smiled. "Why, *thank you*, Robbie. I got a feelin' we gonna be good friends. I'm glad you're hangin' 'round with the Kids now. Come on, you hungry?"

Sure, I'd already had breakfast. Still, I don't know about you, but I can *always* eat. *Two* breakfasts? Why not? It was Saturday. (How many times am I gonna say that?)

After we ordered our food and sat down to eat at a nearby Denny's, I saw that Tanesa had a large smile on her face while chomping down on her croissant breakfast sandwich.

"Hey, Tanesa, you seem pretty happy this morning," I said.

"Ohh," Tanesa said, some crumbles of food dropping out of the corner of her mouth. "I'm always pretty happy. But today, I'm *really* happy."

"How come?" I asked.

"Well," and now she finished chomping before she talked, "let's just say I heard something last night that makes *today* a really special day."

"What'd you hear?" I asked, putting down the last half of my own croissant sandwich and leaning forward, intrigued.

"Mmm," Tanesa said, finishing up her sandwich, "I can't really say anything yet. But, um, you'll know soon enough. It's something *big*, though."

"Big?" I asked, wide-eyed.

"*Really* big."

Her smile somehow got wider, she wiped her hands with her napkin, and she stood up out of her chair. "Come on, Robbie, we got stuff to do."

The next thing I knew, we were *both* up and out of there. (Like I said, Tanesa was *driven* and she moves *fast*.)

Sitting in her living room, I was finishing the rest of my croissant sandwich I'd brought with me, when Tanesa turned to me on the couch to say, "Y'all like scary movies, Robbie?"

Actually, I *don't* like scary movies. Something about them—oh, I don't know—*scares* me. I've tried in the past, but every time I was brave enough to make an attempt, I'd have to stop. Even when friends would put them on at sleepover parties, I'd just leave the room and go read. (Part of why I always bring a book with me to these parties!)

I knew I was making a good impression, though. I knew that Tanesa thought I was a good guy—fun and hopefully even a little funny. I was pretty sure she was seeing I was the kind of dude who could hang around with the Kids of

Widney Junior High. But now this seemed like a test. Was I *brave* enough to hang out with the band?

"Uhhh," I said, trying to remain thoughtful about it. "I ...uh..."

"'Cause I *lovvvvve* scary movies, Robbie," Tanesa said. "Shelly loves all different *kinds* of movies. But me? Mmm mmm. I love the *scary* ones. Real horror stuff. You wanna watch *Nightmare on Elm Street 2*?"

Now, hold on one second.

Here was the *other* problem: not only did scary movies, well, *scare* me, but I wasn't really *supposed* to watch them, either. Sometimes they'd come on when I'd be watching TV and my mom would be busy or working late. And when my friends would put them on at sleepovers, I don't think *any* of us were really *supposed* to be watching them.

But Tanesa seemed to do a *lot* of things her own way, and I guess if she could handle the movies, and her own mom was cool with her watching that stuff, more power to her. She obviously isn't scared of much. Maybe she isn't scared of *anything*. Being the semileader of the band, I guess she needs to be fearless.

Before I could say any of this, though, I was saved by the bell. It was my mom on the phone. She said she'd call when she got back to Tanesa's house to pick me up.

And that was how my phone literally saved me from being attacked by *Nightmare on Elm Street*'s resident monster, Mr. Freddy Krueger.

RINNNNNNG!

RINNNNNNG!

CHAPTER 7

Daniel's On the Air

Aside from getting to know her better, another cool thing that came out of hanging with Tanesa was that she told the other Kids of Widney Junior High members that I'm an "all-right guy." Which meant that they wanted to hang out with me now too.

In fact, it was only a few afternoons later that I was getting my textbooks and some papers out of my locker before heading home when I felt a tap on my shoulder. It was Daniel asking if I'd be up to come home with *him*.

"Sure, Daniel," I said. "My mom has to work late tonight, and it'd be awesome to go to your house instead of having to take the bus. My mom can pick me up after we're done."

"Yes," Daniel said, articulating his words very carefully with a very, very deep voice that made him sound much older than he is. "I think that would be a good idea too."

Because Daniel lives with both blindness and cerebral palsy (like Tanesa), it's nearly impossible for him to walk home on his own. Because his parents and older siblings all have jobs that keep them out until very late in the evening, he can't get a ride with them.

Since he can't stand the school bus any more than I can (what is with the *smell* in that thing?!), he's able to use a special service provided by the city called Access Mobility that is like a private taxi for students like him who deal with movement issues.

I was going to help Daniel walk toward the exit, when he stopped me. He presented me his white-and-red walking cane, before informing me: "Excuse me, Robbie. I do not mean to be rude. I know you are only trying to help. But it is important to know that when you are walking with a person who is blind, it is best to *ask* first if he or she needs guidance."

"Oh, man," I said, slapping my forehead. "I didn't even think of that. It was a reflex."

"I know, Robbie," Daniel said without smiling. (I'd later learn that Daniel is a nice enough guy but doesn't really smile that often.) "You were only trying to be a good friend. But in this case, being a good friend means *asking permission* to guide me. And, no thank you, I can get by for now on my own."

As we walked side by side—Daniel using his cane for guidance and me lugging my backpack filled with textbooks and paper—I asked Daniel if Cain mostly preferred to get around on his own too, since he also lives with blindness.

"Cain is his own person," Daniel said. "I do think it is important to ask *any* person who is blind or person with disability if he or she would like you to help before you start doing it. Also, just because Cain is blind and I happen to be blind too, this does not mean we both think the same way about everything. We are *very* different people."

"That makes sense," I said, almost reaching over to the door to open it for Daniel . . . before he got there first and opened it for *me*.

"You first," he said.

I went through the doorway, and a gaggle of girls went through too, saying, "Thanks, Daniel!"

Daniel said, "No problem" to them, and they smiled on their way out, passing by me on their way out to the school bus on the black asphalt parking lot beyond the grassy yard in front of us.

After Daniel came out, he closed the door and then continued walking, pointing his cane at the parking lot. "The Access Mobility car is bright blue and should say 'Access Mobility' on the side in white letters. It should be here any minute. Although, a lot of the time, they are late."

It was a smooth and quiet ride in the comfy Access Mobility car. I think it may have been a Prius. I have to admit, I was a little jealous that Daniel gets to have his own private taxi of a sort to take him to school and home. He can even use it a few times a week to go to the store or other places if they're within a certain distance.

When I brought this up to Daniel, he said I shouldn't feel bad about being envious like that. He's very glad there are services out there like Access Mobility for people with disabilities, and they do definitely make life a whole lot easier for people like him. So, of course I'd be jealous. It just makes sense.

Daniel likes to talk about things "making sense." For him, logic and reason are extremely important. It's almost as though he's always doing math in his head, figuring out the way the world works. I really liked that about Daniel as I got to know him better.

There is no doubt that Daniel is the smartest of the Kids of Widney Junior High members. He's probably the smartest person I've ever met.

He really showed off his stuff that day when we got to his house and went up to his room. He's set up an entire series of audio engineering doohickeys and whatnot there. It's quite impressive: speakers, microphones, wires going all over the place.

Then there's some stuff I'd never seen or heard of before. I couldn't even tell you now what they are. But man, it's all so elaborate! And it's all for Daniel's podcast show that he produces every day after school.

Daniel had me sit down on his bed while he set his cane down, then sat down on his chair that has wheels at the bottom. He rolled his chair over to his desk and turned on all his doohickeys and whatnot—and they whirred and buzzed, and one thing even vibrated. (I have *no idea* what it was.)

Daniel motioned to me to be quiet, and then he started his show. Which was basically him talking for an hour about all different kinds of things.

Because Daniel enunciates so well and because he has a deep and booming voice, I realized that of *course* he'd be a perfect host and producer of a podcast.

Daniel talked about some things going on with local politics, stuff happening at the school, a few thoughts on some budget cuts to a special-ed program at a *different* school nearby, and what he thought about a particular episode of the show *Speechless*.

I couldn't believe everything he was saying; he was so good at it! I'm not used to friends of mine being so articulate and intelligent.

Where did he get all those words from? How did he know all that stuff? I was amazed that Daniel could be the member of a kick-butt rock-and-roll band like the Kids of Widney Junior High *and* be able to host and produce his own podcast ... while knowing so many different facts and figures and statistics and whatever else to make it the great show it is.

After he covered the local topics and personal opinions, he moved onto the Big News.

This must have been what Tanesa had been keeping from me on Saturday.

"And now, before I end the show, I have some very intriguing news," Daniel said.

Although he *said* it was "intriguing" news, Daniel didn't seem that excited about it. Regardless, he went to say, "My music group, the Kids of Widney Junior High, will be performing in one month at the Key Club on Sunset Blvd. It will be a family-friendly, all-ages show, and we hope you'll all come. Especially since ... we've learned a big producer from one of the top record labels will be attending . . . and is interested in signing our band to his label."

I couldn't believe it! I wanted to scream out with joy. But Daniel, instinctively knowing I'd be excited like that, turned in his wheelie desk chair to me and forcefully shook his head before I could get any sound out.

Then he turned back to his microphone, gave some of the specifics about the upcoming concert, and closed out the episode with a really fantastic outro.

He turned everything off and swiveled his chair back to me.

"Well, what did you think?"

"You were incredible, Daniel," I said.

"Thanks."

"But there's one thing I don't understand," I confessed. "You said you guys might get signed to a big label. Why aren't you more excited about the news?"

"Well," Daniel said, sighing. "I have to tell you, Robbie. I love being in the Kids of Widney Junior High . . ."

"Yeah . . . ?"

"But sometimes, I cannot help but wonder: Do people really like our music . . . or do they only come and cheer us on because they feel bad for us?"

Geez. I never thought of it like that before.

"I mean, think about our *name*, Robbie," Daniel said. "The *Kids* of Widney Junior High. Right now, maybe that's all right. But if the band keeps going, let's say, and we're in our twenties or even thirties, will people still think of us as . . . *kids*?"

"Sure, I can see that being a problem, Daniel," I ventured. Then I couldn't help myself: "But the Beach Boys are still called the Beach *Boys* even though they're all *way* older than 'boys' now. And the Beastie Boys had the same thing right up till the end too. They didn't change *their* names as they got older. Or think of the Get Up Kids or the Cold War Kids, the Indigo Girls, heck or what about the comedy group the Kids in the Hall?"

I realized maybe I was stepping out of line here, so I stopped short. *Had* I gone too far? Who was *I* to contradict Daniel here, and after all—

"Gosh, you know something, Robbie?" Daniel said. "You're a pretty smart guy. I like the way you think."

Phew! I guess we *both* were making good points. I could tell right then, though, that I *had* made the right decision in giving Daniel my own opinion on the matter ... even if it was different than his own. I guess he respected that I spoke up and even what I had to say.

The important thing was that obviously, *I* thought the Kids' music was great. Going to their rehearsal, listening to their demos at home ... but then I was just me, and who knew why other people might be into them. I hoped it was because they really liked the band and the music and not because they "felt bad," like Daniel worried.

I would find out soon enough.

CHAPTER 8

How Peewee and Elisa Met

But first . . . a bit more of my favorite part so far about hanging out with the Kids: *those rehearsals!*

By the end of the week, I had already attended three more rehearsals in Mr. Monagan's garage. Mr. Monagan had told everyone that with the Key Club show coming up soon, they needed to practice as much as possible.

After Mr. Monagan made his declaration about the extra rehearsals, Shelly made a joke, saying, "Practice makes perfect, Michael. But none of us are perfect, and we're never gonna be."

I couldn't help but chuckle at the notion, before I noticed Shelly wasn't laughing and the other Kids members were nodding their heads in approval.

Mr. Monagan nodded his head too, saying with a gentle smile, "That's very true, Shelly. But we're not practicing to be perfect. We're practicing to be *ready*."

Everyone appeared to agree, including yours truly. Wow, Mr. Monagan was *always* able to put everything in such simple terms without being too . . . well, simplistic!

So, anyway: rehearsal #4.

The Kids were finishing up a rowdy rendition of one of my four favorite songs of theirs, "Act Your Age," from their third album of the same name. I was watching from an old, yellow, plush loveseat Mr. Monagan has in the corner of his garage. The garage was not too cold but *did* smell musty.

The music was the best I've ever heard live. Then I noticed something.

Every time I'd seen a rehearsal, Peewee and Elisa would end up standing next to each other. Holding hands. The more I thought about it, the more I realized they're *always* holding hands onstage.

I was still thinking about it while we were waiting for everyone's parents to pick them up. Cain got a ride with his older sister (who is the one who mainly takes care of him, even though he lives with his mother and her boyfriend, neither of whom speak any English).

"Ayyyy, *muchacho!*" Peewee crowed at me. "I got a penny for your thoughts, if you want one."

I smiled wide at Peewee and told him he doesn't have to pay me for my thoughts. "I was just wondering why Elisa and you always seem to end up together on stage . . . and stuff."

"And . . . *stuff, muchacho?*" Peewee smirked.

"Well, you know," I stammered, "like how you guys . . . *hold HANDS* up there all the time. Are you two . . . ?"

"We've been together for a little while now . . ." Elisa stepped over to me from where she was sitting in a yellow plastic chair over by Mr. Monagan, who was fiddling around with a few rock chords on his powder-blue Fender.

"Little, *nothin'!*" Peewee grinned broadly to say. "I feel like we've been *married* for fifteen years, *Bomba!*"

Elisa laughed and playfully tapped Peewee on the right shoulder. Peewee laughed too, and they hugged one another.

"I've never had a girlfriend or anything like that before," I couldn't help but say. As soon as I said it, it felt irrelevant. What would *these* guys care about that? But then I was glad I said it, because it confirmed once again that I could say just about anything I wanted to my new friends. Especially when Peewee turned back to me to say:

"Don't you worry, *muchacho*. You're still just a kid, you know? When you get to be my age, well . . . I'm sure you'll find the right person."

He placed his hand on my shoulder, and for a moment I got a sense that Peewee was starting to become something of an older brother to me. But that would be weird, wouldn't it?

Besides, we look nothing alike!

"You're only a *little* older than Robbie, Luis," Elisa said to Peewee, referring to him as she sometimes would by his real name. (He has *four* of them! Not including his last name!)

"There's that word 'little' again," Peewee said, rubbing the arm of the thick neon pink jacket Elisa was wearing while they waited for her dad to pick them up. "In the future, we should always be using *BIG WORDS!* Big, big, big! *El grrrrraaaannnndeeee!*"

"That's enough, Luis," Elisa said, shaking her head but with a big enough (or should I say *grande* enough?) smile on her face to assure him she was having a good time with all of this. I could only imagine what it must be like to be the girlfriend of a character as larger than life as Peewee!

"Do you want to know the story of how we became girlfriend and boyfriend, Robbie?" Elisa asked, looking at me while rubbing Peewee's buzzed head slowly.

"Sure!"

That was how Elisa unfolded for me the romantic tale of how the two new pals of mine ended up together . . .

ELISA: Peewee and I were only in fourth grade at the time. We were in the same classes a lot because we were in the special-ed program at school. Peewee's two years older than I am, but we would end up being part-nered a lot when we'd be put into reading groups and things, since our last names start with a letter close to each other.

PEEWEE: That's right. Alphabetically, our last names are bumpin' up right next to each other!

ELISA: Peewee, please. I . . . uh, I'm telling the story, okay?

PEEWEE: Whoo-weeee! Okay, Bomba! You're telling the story!

ELISA: Sorry about that, Robbie.

ROBBIE: That's okay, Elisa. So how did you guys

end up actually . . . um, together?

ELISA: We kept getting partnered up, and then one time in a health class, which was part of our PE class, we had to do this mock marriage project.

ROBBIE: Mock marriage?

PEEWEE: FAKE BEING MARRIED, BUDDY!

ROBBIE: Ohhhh.

ELISA: Peewee, seriously. Please, I want to tell the rest of the story and, uh . . . you're . . . you're not helping. Okay? My dad will be here any second, and I want to finish . . .

PEEWEE: Bommmmmba!

ROBBIE: Go ahead, Elisa.

ELISA: So, we had to do this project where Peewee was my . . . uh, husband—but MOCK husband, okay?— and I was his mock wife, of course. And it was a great project, and we got a B+ on it, and our coach was teaching the class since it was really a PE class—

PEEWEE: COACH! Love that guy. Miss him.

ELISA: Y-y-yeah, Luis. I miss him too. But please, I wanna finish now. My dad just texted me and said he's right around the corner and to be ready. [*Elisa turned back to me at this point.*] So, Coach kept making fun of us. In a nice way; he was always nice. But he was teasing us that we were really married and all that . . . and I took it seriously. And after Peewee and I had spent all this time together for our project, and all the jokes Coach was making, I decided to ask Peewee if he wanted to be with me in that way, to be my boyfriend.

And he said YES!!!

For the first time since I'd known him, I saw Peewee looking bashful. His cheeks flushed, and he was clearly somewhat uncomfortable. So, I asked him if he was all right, and he said, "Yeeeeeah, *hombre*. Just all this lovey-dovey mush stuff. Not really for me."

"It's for *me, Luis!*" Elisa said, stomping her foot in a funny way.

From then on, I'd notice that they kept up this kind of running gag together that reminded me of sitcom husbands and wives from some of the old TV shows from the eighties I would watch sometimes with my mom, like *Married . . . with Children* and *Roseanne*. Maybe even the *really* old shows I used to watch through reruns that aired sometimes on the weekends, like *All in the Family*.

Mr. Monagan popped up from his chair like he was launched from a spring when someone knocked at the garage door. He plopped down his guitar and called out to Peewee and Elisa, "That must be Elisa's dad, guys. Great practice today!"

By now, everyone else had been picked up. My mom would be a bit late, which Mr. Monagan had okayed before I came to the rehearsal. So, on their way out, I asked Elisa, "Hey, but what happened to Coach?"

"Oh, that's a story for another day, buddy," Peewee said, shaking my hand on his way out the door.

"Yeah," Elisa confirmed, "or you can read about it in my autobiography. I've been working on it for three years now, and there's plenty about Coach in there."

Before Elisa and Peewee were totally through the door, though, I had to call back out, "Wait, you wrote an *autobiography*, Elisa?"

"Yeah, it's almost seven hundred pages by now! I'll try to get you a copy at one of the next rehearsals. See ya!"

The door was closed. Peewee and Elisa were gone.

I turned to Mr. Monagan at his chair, back to fooling around on his guitar, eyes shut and enjoying the music coming out of his small black-box speaker on the floor.

"Seven hundred pages?" I asked.

Mr. Monagan didn't look up, didn't open his eyes. Just kept smiling and playing, slowly nodding his head in affirmation. "Seven hundred pages."

CHAPTER 9

Sometimes It All Goes Bad

Elisa did manage to get me a copy of her autobiography, and over the next few days, I couldn't put it down—which is saying a *lot*, because the *book* is a lot. It's massive!

When she said it was more than seven hundred pages, she wasn't exaggerating. I mean, I don't know about you, but the longest thing I've ever written was *maybe* ten pages, and that was after I spent a week grounded from using any devices after I'd smarted off to my mom. (It was *Mom's* idea to write a short story over the week after school, when I asked her what I was supposed to do with all that free time.)

But seven hundred pages? The dang thing was *heavy!*

I know a lot of kids these days like to read things on their phones, but for some reason I have trouble with reading things on screens. My mom and my uncle always make fun of me for being an "old soul," and bring up stuff like this a lot to prove their point. I guess I'd rather read actual books and turn pages than stare at a glowing screen that can hurt my eyes or give me a headache. Plus, with an actual real-life book, you get that great "book smell" I love so much!

Also, I prefer the original *Rocky and Bullwinkle Show* to *Pokémon,* but I guess that's my being an "old soul" thing again.

Maybe this also has something to do with why I'm an avowed "misfit" and all and ended up hanging out with a group of friends like the Kids of Widney Junior High!

ANYway, I was poring over the many anecdotes in Elisa's life story for days during class, whenever I had some free time. Imagine how long her book would have been if she were in her twenties. Or even thirties! We're talking *thousands* of pages, dude!

Sure, there were a few times when my teachers caught me reading her massive book when I shouldn't have been (a few pages here or there, snuck out of my backpack). But for the most part, they were cool with this. It's not like I was playing games on my phone.

Truth be told, I've gotten in trouble in the past for reading during class, even at my old school. What can I say? Math and science have their place, but when I'm immersed in a good story like Elisa's, well, that ends up coming first. I'll confess: *I'm an addict for the written word!*

One thing that bothered me about Elisa's book, though, was that she kept bringing up some of the ways that Peewee—who is supposed to be her boyfriend, remember—could be mean to her.

It was clear from the book and from all the time we had been spending together that Peewee truly cares about Elisa, definitely as much as she cares about him. But it was also clear from everything I was reading that Peewee's teasing of Elisa—the same I'd see in person from time to time—did bother her.

Don't get me wrong: Elisa is pretty tough too. She can take care of herself and, even with her disabilities, can handle almost any challenge that comes her way. She's no victim, and she'd be the first to tell you that (as she does on page 432 of her book!).

But yeah, it can't be easy to have someone you're so close to like Peewee poking fun at you so often.

Even though it wasn't really my business, I decided to ask Peewee and Elisa about it during their next band rehearsal.

"Hey, Peewee," I began, "I've been reading Elisa's awesome autobiography . . ."

"Yeah?" he said. "Ooooh, that's good. My *Bomba* is a good writer!"

"You haven't even *read* any of it yet, Antonio!" Elisa said, playfully whacking him on the elbow with her tiny balled-up fist and using one of Peewee's other first names, as she was wont to do.

Cain, Shelly, and Tanesa looked up from where they were going over some of Mr. Monagan's riffs on the guitar, while Daniel was reading a social studies textbook in braille. (Braille, by the way, is a language used by people who are blind, in which they can actually *feel* the words and sentences they're going over by using these rows of miniscule dots that pop up all over the page. Daniel's been teaching me how to read it, and I think I'm getting pretty good at it!)

"Hey, Elisa, p-p-p-please be n-n-nice to Peewee, okay?" Cain said. "Okay, Elisa? Please be nice."

"Ohhhh, she's just playing around," Peewee said to Cain. "We're always playing around like that. A whack to the elbow ain't gonna do me no harm, *hombre*."

"Actually, that's what I wanted to ask you about, if you don't mind, Peewee," I said. "There's a lot in Elisa's book about how when you, um, you know . . . 'play around' with Elisa. Sometimes it makes her feel bad, and she doesn't really know how to tell you."

Now Mr. Monagan looked up too. Daniel stopped reading his textbook and was paying attention to our private conversation. "Everything all right over there, guys?" Mr. Monagan asked.

"Yyyyyeah," Elisa sputtered, seeming unsure. "Robbie's just . . . bringing up some stuff in my book—"

"—Is that *true, gruñir?*" Peewee asked. (I later looked up *gruñir* in my Spanish-English language dictionary at home and saw it means something like "groan," which doesn't really make sense to me when Peewee calls Elisa that, but I guess maybe that's the whole point? Peewee definitely has his own way of talking, sorta like Cain, and I'm not going to butt into *that* situation at all!)

Elisa turned to Peewee and, looking down at her shoes, timidly admitted that, yes, there are times when he's "obviously just having some fun" but that it can be "a bit much."

"I really like you, Peewee," Elisa said. "And I like how funny you are. But . . . well, I need you to be more sensitive to how what you say can affect me and my mood. Okay?"

I looked to Mr. Monagan, whose large grin somehow grew even larger. He seemed very proud of Elisa for sticking up for herself, and I was too. It's not easy to stand your ground and tell someone how what they're saying or doing might be making you feel. Especially when he or she is a close friend.

"See that, everybody?" Mr. Monagan affirmed. "Elisa telling Peewee exactly how she's feeling is so important. Otherwise, how can he know what she's going through? Communication is key, my friends. Communication is key."

And then Mr. Monagan went back to fiddling around on his guitar, while Shelly and Tanesa watched and listened. Daniel went back to his book. But Cain shuffled closer to where I was with Elisa and Peewee. Cain had a worried expression on his face.

"B-b-but it's not enough to say you f-f-f-eel bad, Elisa," Cain said. "Peewee, are you g-g-g-gonna say you're sorry?"

Elisa looked to Peewee. Peewee looked to Elisa. Then he looked to . . . *me*. "Wellllll . . . ," he said. "I'm just playin' around, Cain. And Elisa knows that. Right, *gruñir?*"

"That's *it!*" Elisa stamped her feet, breaking away from Peewee's warm grasp. "Peewee Luis Antonio Fernando, I have had *enough* of you for one day! I tell you how I feel, and you still don't listen. Our new friend Robbie even brings up how he sees what you do to me sometimes in my book, and you don't listen. Enough, enough, *enough!*"

And with that, Elisa ran up the stairs and went out the

door to Mr. Monagan's living room, noisily slamming it behind her.

"Uh, oh," Mr. Monagan said, standing and going up the stairs after Elisa. "Hold on, guys. Everyone stay put for a minute."

In opening the door again, though, Mr. Monagan's fat, gray, old cat Fievel scrambled out from where he was being kept inside and charged down the stairs, knocking Mr. Monagan backward.

With the cat mewling angrily on its dash down the stairs, Mr. Monagan barely caught himself on the banister with his right arm, nearly toppling down entirely.

"Oh, geez," I said, watching as the pandemonium continued, with Shelly and Tanesa and Daniel getting into the act and all talking loudly over one another, yelling at Peewee for causing Elisa to run off.

If that wasn't enough commotion already, in backing away from them all, Peewee tripped on a wire, and one of the small black amps sparked, causing a slight electrical fire. *POP! POP!*

"OH, GEEZ!" I said louder this time, rushing to the fire, unplugging the amp from the wall, and spraying it with Mr. Monagan's extinguisher before throwing a blanket on it that was nearby.

The fire went out quickly and easily, but not before Fievel the cat began running around shrieking in circles like a banshee.

Oh, geez, oh, geez, oh, geeeez!!

Daniel angrily slammed his textbook shut. "Well, *I'm* clearly not getting my homework done here. Could someone please call Access Mobility to come pick me up and take me home? I'm outta here!"

"Yeah, me too!" Cain cried out, louder than I'd ever heard him talk before. It was so loud, in fact, that everyone now turned his or her attention to Cain. It seemed even Fievel the cat was watching and waiting.

Cain was *never* loud or upset, but here he was, looking more fiery than the tiny blaze I'd put out moments earlier.

"I'm mad, okay?!" Cain cried out, scrunching his face, his nut-brown skin growing rose red. "P-p-peewee is being mean to Elisa! Elisa is running off! Daniel wants to leave now, t-t-too! *I'm very mad, okay?!*"

Mr. Monagan hobbled down the stairs, having found his balance from the near fall. He went to Cain and placed his calm hand on Cain's shoulder. "Hey, pal, you gonna be all right? Let's do some breathing exercises . . ."

"No! No, Mr. Monagan! No br-br-br-breathing exercises!" Cain turned away from Mr. Monagan, so enraged I couldn't believe it. Cain was always the lovable teddy bear of the group, and now . . . I didn't know *what* to think.

I had to remember that everyone has different sides to their personalities and that Cain is most certainly *not* a teddy bear; he is a young man just like me, and we all have our breaking points!

"I'm l-l-l-eaving, too!" Cain hollered.

"Okay, Cain," Mr. Monagan said. "I'll call your sister Patti and have her come get you early . . ."

"No! No, Mr. Monagan!" Cain continued. "I'm leaving th-th-the *band.* I can't do this no more!"

Now I was almost *certain* that Fievel the cat was gaping at Cain, just as we all were.

"You're leaving the . . . *band*, Cain?" Shelly asked in disbelief. "You can't do that. We're a . . . *family*."

"No. No, Shelly! I'm s-s-s-orry, but I can't do this no more," Cain said. "And b-b-b-besides, my family needs me. My cousin is having another baby, and my family needs someone to take her place and help sweep and clean up at our b-b-b-bodega after school. I can't k-k-k-keep coming to rehearsals. *They're* my family. N-n-not the Kids of Widney Junior High!"

There was an awed silence in the room. Everyone was pondering Cain's announcement.

"I'm . . . s-s-s-sorry," Cain said, calming down. "It was something I was gonna bring up a-f-f-fter our big show at Key Club. But you know what? Now's as g-g-g-good a time as any to tell you—I'm quitting the band."

We all looked to Mr. Monagan, whose large grin for the first time ever was nowhere to be seen. He didn't say anything at first. Then: "I tell you what, gang: Lemme call everyone's parents to pick them up. We'll figure this out tomorrow."

"Looks like we have a *lot* to figure out, Michael!" Tanesa said.

Oh, geez!

CHAPTER 10

After the Aftermath
(Part One)

Ohhhhhh geeeeeeeezzz!!

Let me quickly catch you up to where we are now in the story:

The big Kids of Widney Junior High Key Club show is only two weeks away. There's a serious possibility that the record producer who will be in the audience might sign the Kids if they put on a killer show. That could be a life-changing development for the band and Mr. Monagan and the Kids as individuals.

Meanwhile . . . Elisa got so mad at Peewee, after his reaction to her sometimes feeling bad when he teases her, that she doesn't want to come to rehearsals anymore. Peewee feels *so* bad about this whole thing that he hasn't been his usual bubbly, energetic self. It's been kind of sad to watch, to be honest.

Sitting at the lunch table with Shelly, Tanesa, and Daniel, we all watched remorsefully as Peewee slowly—like a robot—shoved his peanut butter and jelly sandwiches into his mouth, one by one, until all nine were gone.

He didn't look like he was enjoying them, and I can tell you, seeing Peewee eating all those peanut butter and jelly sandwiches without enjoying them was *truly* a sad, sad sight. (Especially since—*come ON!*—who can eat a peanut butter and jelly sandwich without smiling? Particularly when there's *nine* of them?)

Now, I know what you're wondering: *But where was Cain during these sad lunchtime sessions?* Cain, as you'll recall, quit the band entirely. Elisa simply stopped showing up for rehearsals. Was she still in the band? Who knew? She wasn't talking to any of us, and even Mr. Monagan was leaving her alone to, once again, "figure it out on her own."

But Cain? Dude was *done*.

After his uncharacteristic explosion at that fateful rehearsal almost a week earlier, he too refused to talk with any of us. As soon as school was over at the end of the day, he would take an Access Mobility car straight to his uncle's grocery store, where he helped sweep and clean. Then he'd go home to his mom's house with his sister Patti, eat his *frijoles* and tamales that his mom always makes, and go straight to sleep.

That routine became Cain's day. And, frankly, I found *that* to be kind of sad too. No more fun and laughter with the Kids at rehearsals? It was hard to watch, man.

I knew that Elisa missed spending time with the band.

I could tell, every time I saw her in the halls with her head down, lugging around her huge, purple-and-red book bag on her back, always overfilled with papers poking out of the partway-zippered sides. Sometimes she'd look up at me and try to grant me a smile. But most of the time, she kept her eyes on her bright-yellow shoes that reminded me of tennis balls.

Cain I *knew* missed being in the band even if he no longer wanted to put up with all the "nonsense," as he put it in a letter I got from one of his classroom aides:

Hola, ¿qué tal?, my good friend, Robbie.

I am sorry that I haven't been coming by to you to say hola, ¿qué tal?, at lunch like I used to. And I am sorry I am not coming to rehearsals at Mr. Monagan's house no more or am in the band.

Peewee is my good friend too, but he has not been very good to Elisa sometimes, and I am very mad that even when she tells him this, thanks to you bringing it up to him at that rehearsal, he still is not as nice as he could be.

Being in the band is supposed to be about being good to each other, and spreading happiness and love. And that's not what it's been like ever since we started practicing so hard for the big show at the end of the month.

I miss you very much and am missing the singing. But right now I am needing to be spending some time by myself and keep helping out my uncle and my family at our grocery store.

Thank you for understanding and for being my very good friend.

Your very, very good friend, Cain.

Everyone was in such a tizzy that even Daniel was having trouble producing his podcast. He had started doing them later in the evening to make up for his constant practicing with the band, but the routine was clearly wearing him out.

Daniel was also still wondering if signing to a label would be a good idea, and whether or not they were doing all of this just to make people feel better about themselves for coming and seeing "those poor retarded kids singing up on stage," as he put it.

When I tried to explain to Daniel that there was no way that's what people who came to their shows were thinking, Peewee finally looked up from his eighth peanut butter and jelly sandwich to say the first thing he'd said in days: "Well, *muchacho*, I tell you what: People come to our shows for many different reasons. Some people come because they love our music. Some people because they connect with our special lyrics about being special kids. You know what? Some people come because they think we're funny, which is okay too. And some people, sure, *muchacho*, they come because *maybe* they feel bad for us. But that's okay! As long as they're coming and having a good time, it doesn't matter."

Shelly agreed, bringing up a documentary he'd seen about a musician named Daniel Johnston, whom he really liked. "You know, when I watched the documentary movie about Daniel Johnston, I could see that people went to *his* shows for a lot of the same reasons they come to *our* shows. Daniel Johnston had some special things about *himself* too, some pretty serious mental problems, I think. But he still made the music that pleased his crowds. And they went to his shows because they liked his music, they liked his lyrics, they maybe found the whole thing funny, or even because they felt bad for Daniel Johnston. But they would go and were always really happy. And that made Daniel Johnston . . . very . . . happpppppy."

"I'll have to see that documentary," *our* Daniel said. "Especially since this guy sounds like he had a lot in common with us. Especially *me!*"

Our Daniel granted us a rare smile (he's usually so, *so* serious), and we all laughed. Peewee asked if any of us wanted his last sandwich. When we said we were full, he chucked it up at the ceiling (*PLOP!*), and it never came back down.

It was Tanesa's idea for us to all go see Cain at his grocery store after school. She told Mr. Monagan what we were going to do, and he agreed it was not a bad thought. We'd still try to make it to rehearsal after, but for now, all of us, except for Peewee, who wasn't "feeling up to it," were all off to the little store, or *bodega*, as Cain had called it in the past, by his house in the deepest part of East LA.

The Access Mobility driver was nice enough to let me hitch a ride with the Kids of Widney Junior High members again. Now, I did feel a little bad that I was using something that was meant for people who have special limitations

and need the transportation. But Tanesa told me that sometimes her sister or even mother would come along with her, and it's not a big deal as long as the car or van isn't full. "An empty seat is an empty seat!" she said. "Your tax dollars at work, Robbie! Every time y'all buyin' somethin' at the store, y'all got the sales tax. And part of that goes to Access, so it's all good, y'know."

I *guess* that made me feel better. A little bit, at least. Or something.

Then again, I *had* to go with the Kids to go see Cain. He'd written me that letter (or at least orated it aloud to his classroom aide, who'd typed it up for him), and it was clear I would be of some help in talking with him with everyone else. No one else had gotten a letter from him is what I mean.

The Access Mobility van—which was equipped with various buckles on the floor for people's wheelchairs, rattling as we drove around through the neighborhood to Cain's bodega, with a lot of signs in Spanish—smelled like some kind of cleaning liquid, like the kind of smell you'd smell in a hospital or doctor's office. Clean but, like, *chemical* clean.

To be honest, I was glad to get out of the van once we arrived at Cain's family's grocery store. I'm glad there's a service for people who need it, but that smell. It was overpowering. And this time, the driver seemed a little mean. There were times when he took turns a little too fast, and when I asked Tanesa, who was sitting next to me, about it in a whisper, she whispered back, "That's how they is sometimes, and ain't nothin' we can do about it, Robbie!"

I guess you get what you pay for.

Shelly said they were writing a song about just this problem (that some of the Access drivers aren't very nice). But we had something else to deal with as we walked into Cain's grocery store with a jingle at the door.

Long story short: *it didn't go well.*

Cain smiled when he heard us coming in. But only for a moment.

There he was in his green apron, propping himself up on the end of a large, dirty broom he was using to sweep through the aisles crowded with canned tomatoes and black beans and salsas and various fruits and vegetables. *SWISH SWISH SWISH!* went his large broom.

Cain turned away from us: "I asked you guys f-f-f-for s-s-s-s-some time alone, please."

"Come on, Cain," Tanesa said, stepping toward him. "You're not gonna miss the big ol' show comin' up. We need you in the band. You sing 'Respect,' which everyone knows is one of our best songs."

"Yeah, Cain," Shelly tried. "You can't leave *now*. What about all the time we put into our *band*? It's a *band*, Cain. You can't leave the *band*. We're a *band*. Band, band . . . *bannnnnnnnd.*"

"No!" Cain said, sweeping faster away from us. *SWISH SWISH SWISH!*

Daniel, with a little help being sight-guided by me with his hand on my shoulder, gave it a shot: "Hi, Cain. This is Daniel."

Cain stopped and waited. "*Hola, ¿qué tal?*, Daniel. Hello, my good, my very good friend, Daniel."

"Look, I . . . understand what you're going through and thinking about, Cain. I . . . I've been having similar struggles deciding if I want to stay in the band or not, and whether or not what we're doing is a *good* thing . . . or maybe it's something that's not really *helping* the image of people with disabilities—"

"Cain!" we heard from behind the dirty plastic stripping of the barrier between the store and the backroom. "*Te necesitamos en la parte de atrás ahora mismo.*"

"Th-th-that's my *tío* in the back," Cain told us without turning around. "I need to . . . I need to get back there. I'm n-n-not working here to talk. I'm working here to w-w-w-work."

"*Bien, mi tío amigo favorito,*" Cain called out to his uncle or, as I was learning, his *tío*.

"*Necesitamos hacer tus pruebas de azúcar,*" Cain's *tío* could be heard yelling out from the back.

"*Also,*" Cain sputtered, not turning around to us, "it's t-t-t-time for m-m-my sugar test. Sugar test. Time to t-t-t-test my sugars."

And with that, Cain used the sweeping broom as a guided stick to get himself to the backroom—*SWISH SWISH SWISH!*—disappearing through the dirty plastic stripping hanging from the ceiling.

Daniel, using me to help him turn back to Tanesa, Peewee, and Shelly, said it best: "Well, we tried."

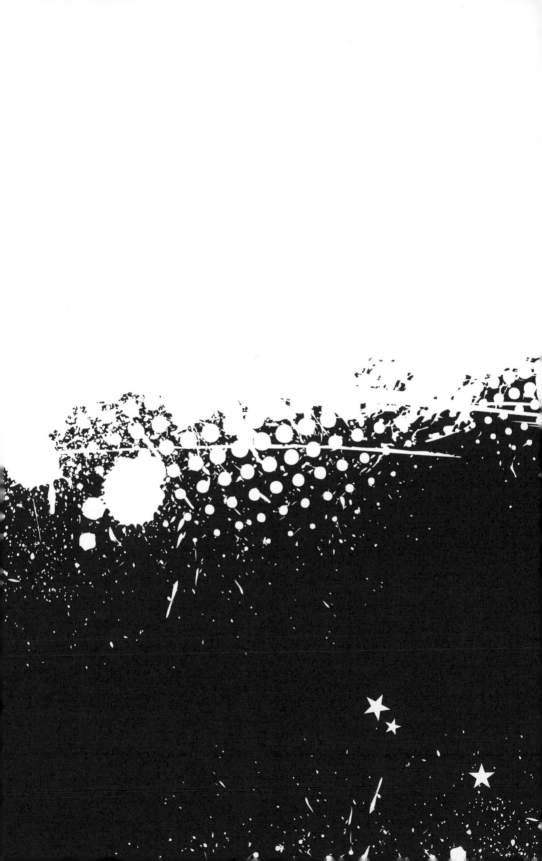

CHAPTER 11

After the Aftermath
(Part Two)

Do you ever meditate?

Whenever I'm really stressed out, like when I'm feeling too much pressure from school or anything else (or when a bunch of my friends are fighting with each other like the Kids were!), I'll sit down, cross my legs, relax, loosen my shoulders, roll my neck around a little, close my eyes, straighten my spine, and, yeah, *meditate*.

It's simpler than it sounds, with the hardest part being just sitting there with your eyes closed, breathing slowly innnnnnn and breathing slowly outtttttttt.

I highly recommend it to anyone who's feeling nervous or scared, anxious or worried, angry or frustrated. It's so easy when you're feeling like that to just go online and say a bunch of mean things on Twitter or Instagram or something like that. It's just as easy to sit down and watch Netflix or eat a bunch of chocolate cake or something.

Trust me, *I do that too sometimes!*

But I find I feel *soooooo* much better when I meditate.

It might seem tough to just *sit there* with your eyes closed, legs crossed, and trying not to think of anything. But that's why they call it your "practice."

Kind of like when the Kids of Widney Junior High have *practice* for their songs. It's actually pretty similar. You *practice* music the way you *practice* your meditation, or the way you or maybe your parents or older brothers or sisters go and work out at the gym, which is kind of like a workout *practice* for their muscles.

In fact, just like any other practice, I find the more I *practice* my meditation, the better I get at it too. I started with two minutes—just two minutes!—when I first got into it. It was tough, but I did it. After a few weeks, I started meditating for five minutes. Now I'm almost up to ten minutes every time I meditate. It feels so good to get better and better at it the more I do it.

That's what I was doing on the morning I got a phone call from Tanesa saying she and Elisa were going to be watching a movie at her house, and asking if I wanted to join.

Which is how, after spending my Saturday morning meditating, trying to relax, reading a good novel I'd been into for the previous few weeks, and talking things out a little about what had been going on with my new friends in the band with my mom . . . I ended up spending the afternoon at Tanesa's watching . . .

Oh, geez! Another scary movie!!

For some reason, Tanesa couldn't seem to get enough.

I was trying my best not to seem too frightened whenever the monster jumped out of the bushes or whatever it might be, but there was no way Tanesa wouldn't notice that I was super scared.

"*GOOD GOLLY GRAVY!*" I cried out at one point, turning away on the couch between Tanesa and Elisa.

"Are you okay, Robbie?" Elisa asked, placing a gentle hand on my shoulder.

"I'm . . . fine," I was barely able to say.

"Don't you like these movies?" Elisa asked.

"I guess . . . I mean, I like hanging out with you guys, and it's fun watching movies on Saturdays like this," I found myself saying. "But . . ."

"I know," Elisa said, patting me now to help calm me down. "These movies of Tanesa's *can* be a bit much, can't they?"

"What you talkin' 'bout now?" Tanesa said, smirking and turning to Elisa. "Don't listen to her, Robbie. She can't hardly even *see* much of *nothin'* on the screen."

"Now, you know that's not quite true, Tanesa," Elisa said, looking over my shoulder to do so. "I can see fine. The colors and shapes are there, and I can certainly hear what they're saying all right too. But Robbie's right: this movie might be too scary for him. You remember how hard it was when *you* were his age."

"Awww, he's not that much younger than I am," Tanesa said, pausing the movie to pick up the phone, which had started ringing. (*Tanesa's family must be one of the last on the planet to have a landline,* I remember thinking!)

"It's okay, Robbie," Elisa said, patting me again. "We don't have to keep watching the movie if you don't want to. We can do something else like color, or you can help me edit the latest chapter of my autobiography."

RING RING.

"Elisa, it's for you," Tanesa said, passing the phone across my chest to Elisa next to me, with the cream-colored plastic curly cord stretching from Tanesa through me to Elisa.

"Maybe it's Peewee!" Elisa said, before my eyebrows raised and Tanesa shook her head no. Elisa snatched the phone from Tanesa, the cord growing taut across my chest as she pulled it toward her ear.

"Hello?" Elisa said before her shoulders dropped. I was able to breathe a little easier because this also made the cord looser. "Oh, hi, Michael. How are you today?"

Elisa placed her hand over the mouthpiece of the phone to whisper to Tanesa and me, "It's Mr. Monagan."

"I *know,*" Tanesa said, laughing. "I'm the one who answered the dang phone!"

"What's up?" I asked. "Is everything okay?"

"What's going on, Michael?" Elisa asked. "Mmm hmm . . . Oh . . . Rrrrright . . . Okay . . . Yeah, I would imagine he can do that . . . All right, I'll ask and I'll let you know what he says at the next rehearsal . . . Ohhhhh, we're just watching some movies right here with Robbie . . . Okay, Michael, I will . . . You too."

She gave the phone back to Tanesa but did so from *behind* me, so that the cord now completely wrapped around me. Without realizing what had happened, Tanesa was about to put the phone back into its cradle on the stand by her side of the couch when I cried out: "Wait!"

"Oh!" Tanesa giggled. "Sorry 'bout that, Robbie." She undid the phone cord around me and placed the phone back where it belonged. *PHEW! (That's why so few people have landlines anymore*, I then thought!)

"Mr. Monagan said to say hi to you, Robbie," Elisa said.

"What was he calling about?" I asked.

"Heeee just wanted to know if my dad could be one of the people to help drive us all to the Key Club show on Friday night," Elisa answered.

"Yeah, I bet he don't want to rely on Access for *that* night!" Tanesa said, exploding in more laughter. "We don't want to risk being late to *that* one."

"Man, I can't believe after all this excitement and everything that's been going on, the Key Club concert is right around the corner now," I said. "That's pretty wild."

"Just another show," Tanesa said, turning the movie back on and facing the screen again—the screen that began *SHRRRRRIIIEEEKING* so loud, I had to cover my ears. Ugh, I *hate, hate, HATE* scary movies!

"Tanesa, please turn it down, girl," Elisa asked. Tanesa did so and turned back to Elisa, with a confused look on her face.

"Hey, what's gotten into you all of a sudden?" Tanesa asked.

"Oh, nothing," Elisa said. "I just thought maybe that would be Peewee. I . . . I miss him."

"Well, the important thing is that you're gonna be playin' in the band with the rest of us at Key Club," Tanesa said. "That was pretty dumb of you to try to stay away while we got this big show comin' up, Elisa. I mean, *come ONNNNNN!*"

"Yeeeeahhh," Elisa said, shifting in her seat, eyes going back and forth between me and the screen—where the monster *AGAIN!* popped out of a bush, making she and I jump. "But I'm still waiting on Peewee to prove to me that he can be nice as a boyfriend. I want him back, but I want him back as a *good* guy and I . . . just don't know if he can really do that as much as I need him to."

"Awwww, Peewee's just Peewee," Tanesa said, turning the volume back up on the screen and facing the TV again: *AAAAUUUUUGGHHHH!!!!!*

I held my hands over my ears, closing my eyes before turning back to Elisa. "Is that all Mr. Monagan was asking about, Elisa? That your dad would be one of the drivers for all the band members that night?"

"Actually . . . now that you ask, *no.*"

"*Uhhhhh* oh," Tanesa said, not turning back to us, eyes locked on the screen. "That don't sound too good."

"Well, it might be a problem," Elisa said. "Mr. Monagan said that he found out that the producer from the record label who's coming . . . his favorite song is . . . 'Respect.'"

"But that's *Cain's* song!" I jumped up, not because of the movie but because the even-larger feeling inside my stomach was forcing me to. "Cain *always* sings that one! It's even his song on the album!"

"I guess we got a problem then, don't we?" Tanesa said,

turning the movie up even louder, maybe as a response to me jumping up and hollering.

"Yeah, but aren't you guys going to do anything about it? We need to get Cain to be at that show that night! It could be your big break!! The Kids of Widney Junior High could finally be on a huge record label and go mainstream! Be on *Jimmy Kimmel* and all that stuff!"

"I guess maybe one of the other Kids like Tanesa or me will have to learn the song," Elisa shrugged.

"AUGGGGGH!!!" shrieked the TV. This time, I didn't even flinch. There was no scary movie, no monster jumping out of a bush for the umpteenth time that could beat me down right then.

That feeling in my stomach was still growing, and I had to say it: "Guys, enough's enough! Elisa, you're all amazing singers, but there's no way you can be the best you can be at that song in less than a few days. It's Cain's song, *period*."

"So, what do you expect us to do, Robbie?" Tanesa said, turning off the TV and movie altogether at last. "You gonna help us go get Cain? We tried once before."

"This time will be different," I said. "Come on, let's go get *everyone*. Even *Peewee*," I said, looking right at Elisa. She looked back at me and slowly nodded. "If Cain understands the *whole band* is there for him, he might change his mind."

"Yeah," Elisa said softly. Then louder: "Yeah!!"

"What we gonna do?" Tanesa asked again.

"No more *trying* to get Cain," I declared. "We're gonna *do it*. Follow me, guys!"

And out the door we went.

And somehow, I was now in charge of getting Cain back in the band and patching up Peewee's and Elisa's boy-friend-girlfriend relationship.

Now how in the heck did *that* happen?

CHAPTER 12

Teamwork Sometimes Breaks Instead

Two days before the big Key Club show.

Things were *not* all good in the world of the Kids of Widney Junior High.

I kept wondering, *How did we get here?* I was also wondering, *How did I end up holding a fried hot dog covered in lemon-flavored whipped cream and banana slices?*

See, in the few days since the scary movie at Tanesa's with Elisa:

(1) I got a B+ on my book report about the comedy stylings of old-school British duo Dudley Moore and Peter Cook. I prefer the original *Arthur* to the new one. The old *Bedazzled* with Moore and Cook was way better than the new one too. Although even the new one isn't that new anymore.

(2) Peewee began bringing egg salad sandwiches to lunch instead of PB&J. He still ate nine of them at a time. I have no idea what that's going to do to his cholesterol level, but I also still keep thinking of Peewee as something of a superhero, so I guess he'll be okay. Even though he tends to smell like garlic and egg farts now, something he seems to actually embrace.

(3) Elisa *tried* coming to one of the rehearsals at Mr. Monagan's garage, but being there with Peewee—even though they were on opposite sides of the practice space—was too much for her, so she left early. Everyone got mad at Peewee for continuing to not step up and apologize once and for all to Elisa for all the teasing in the past. Peewee just belched and it smelled like . . . garlic and egg farts. At that point, *everyone* went to the other side of the practice space, away from Peewee.

(4) So now the band was missing Cain *and* Elisa. We were pretty sure Elisa was still coming to the concert Friday night at least, because she had promised her dad would help drive everyone there. But rehearsals without her just weren't the same. And without Cain, they were *really* not the same. I know I missed hearing "Respect," and we were worried the record producer coming to the concert would too. *Darn it!*

(5) *What to do what to do what to do what to doooooo?!*

(6) Peewee felt so bad about what was happening with Elisa (to his credit, at this point in the game, she wouldn't even meet up to *let* him apologize), he decided to come with me when I told him I was gonna go get Cain back

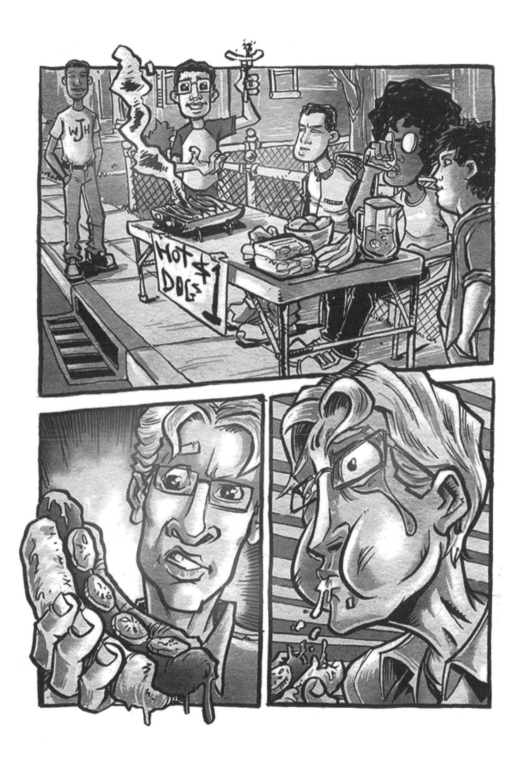

myself. "Tell you what, *hombre*, if I can't get Elisa to come back for rehearsals, at least I can get Cain back for the big show, no?"

(7) It didn't work out.

(8) *Great.* Cain was not only not coming to the show, but now he was mad that Peewee and I had come to try to get him back *uhhhhh-gan.* "I'm mad, okay?!" he had screamed at us, standing over his broom in the grocery store. Peewee and I were so shocked that we didn't know what to say or do except stand there with mouths gaping. Then Peewee belched. And it smelled like . . . PB&J (apparently he'd gone back to his traditional sandwich brand again after enough people had been complaining about the smell).

Which gets us back to two days before the Key Club concert and me standing there on a street corner by Mr. Monagan's house at a table the Kids and I'd set up. Why was I holding a fried hot dog covered in lemon-flavored whipped cream and banana slices?

Shelly had come up with the idea that maybe one way to get Cain back was to try to start our own business and make enough money so he could give some of it to his uncle, which in turn would make up for Cain not working at the grocery store after school.

Right?

Welllllllll . . .

We certainly gave it our all. We only had a few days to get it done, so we tried selling lemonade at our little make-shift stand outside Mr. Monagan's house. A whopping two people came by after five hours of doing our best to sell our pitcher of lemonade, most of which Tanesa had been sneaking sips of until it was almost all gone anyway. *Tanesa!*

Since Daniel was taking a break from his podcast, he thought maybe what we could sell was good advice, the kind he had frequently offered up on his show. Shelly brought up the fact that this was what Lucy from the Charlie Brown gang used to do, and it seemed to work well for *her*.

It didn't work well for *us*.

I think part of the problem was that when the two or three people who came to us asked for advice, Peewee kept saying things like, "Awww, quit yer bellyachin'." That didn't seem to help. *Peewee!*

So I suggested one more thing: hot dogs! We could buy, cook up, and sell hot dogs super-easy. Couldn't we?

Answer: *No. No, we couldn't.*

The hot dogs were not selling. This was a worse disaster than the sour lemonade that Tanesa had been drinking most of (ending up with puckered lips by night's end for her trouble). This was worse than our advice table, which ended up with at least one dissatisfied customer reporting Peewee to the American Psychological Association *and* the Better Business Bureau.

We had been working all week on trying to get Elisa to come to rehearsals, trying to get Cain back in the band, and trying to make money to give to Cain so he'd be tempted to stop working for his uncle at least long enough to come to the concert. And all we ended up with were hot dogs. Which no one wanted to buy.

And *that's* how I ended up standing there behind our table at 4:32 p.m. wondering if maybe we should have served them with mustard and ketchup like they did in most places instead of the lemon-flavored whipped cream and bananas that Shelly had suggested after seeing the combination in a movie from the 1970s he saw late on TV the night before. (Tanesa was the one who had suggested we deep-fry them first, too; don't even ask how we got *that* little task accomplished!)

My hot dog idea had *not* worked out. *Robbie!*

That was around the time that Mr. Monagan came out of his garage to ask us how we were doing. I handed him the deep-fried hot dog covered in lemon-flavored whipped cream and bananas, and said it was on the house. He took it, gave it a huge bite, smiled, waited, and asked with his mouth full if we had a trash can under the table. Luckily, we did.

After Mr. Monagan was done throwing up, he suggested that we had done all we could to get Elisa and Cain back, and maybe now it was time for the Kids to go back to rehearsing again.

"Oh, right, *rehearsing!*" Shelly said, realizing at once what they'd been forgetting all week.

"Ay, Michael's right, everybody," Peewee declared. "Let's ditch all this nonsense and go back to doing what we do best. Let's go sing our brains out, no?"

Everyone cheered, and we realized it was one of those rare instances when Peewee was absolutely right. It *was* time to ditch the nonsense and get back to work!

CHAPTER 13

Peewee Can't Help It

I know what you're wondering.

If we were at Mr. Monagan's house, working with Mr. Monagan on getting the Kids prepped for the big show, why didn't we ask Mr. Monagan to do something about Cain? Cain loves and respects Mr. Monagan, and clearly he'd listen if his *teacher* and band leader asked him to rejoin the group.

Wouldn't he?

But who was going to ask Mr. Monagan to do that? I noticed a few of the Kids were looking suspiciously at me sitting in a purple puffy easy chair while they sang their song "Doctor, Doctor."

Mr. Monagan evidently noticed too. He stopped playing.

"Hey, guys," he asked. "What's going on? You all tired? We need a break?"

"Nahhhh, Michael," Tanesa said, while everyone else stopped singing. It was pretty cool the way they always seemed to know what the other band members were thinking. The Kids are a true team.

"Well, then what is it, Tanesa?" Mr. Monagan asked, picking a few chords on his guitar that reminded me of an Elliott Smith song while we were waiting.

"It's just that ... ummmm," Tanesa began, turning her attention to Daniel, who finished the thought for her:

"Look, Michael, we ... are all wondering what it is we're supposed to do about Cain no longer being in the band ..."

"Ahhhhh, I see," Mr. Monagan said. "That *is* a problem, isn't it?"

He pursed his lips and nodded his head slowly, rocking a little in his wooden rocking chair.

"Right," Daniel continued. "And so we were thinking ... if it wouldn't be too much trouble ... since Cain is your *student* and all, maybe you could ..."

"Could what, Daniel?"

"Could ... possibly, if it would be all right, go to the bodega and ask him to come back into the band. At least long enough so that he can sing 'Respect' at the concert on Friday."

"Ohhhh," Mr. Monagan said, playing a few chords that reminded me more now of Jimi Hendrix. "Mmm hmmm."

"Come on, Michael," Peewee started up. "You know we can't have a show without Cain. And we've tried every which way to get that *jabroni* back onboard with us, no?"

"You have ... I'm well aware," Mr. Monagan said, nodding and rocking gently.

"So, Michael, what do you think?" Shelly asked.

Mr. Monagan kept on nodding and rocking. I'm pretty sure he was playing Nirvana at this point.

"I tell you what," Mr. Monagan said. "Have we talked about the 'dignity of risk' and 'learned helplessness'?"

"Uhhhhh oh," Tanesa giggled. "Here we go again with that mumbo-jumbo talk!"

"No, no, no," Mr. Monagan said, smiling. "It's not mumbo-jumbo, Tanesa. It's good stuff."

"'Dignity of risk'?" Daniel asked, leaning in over his cane. "What's that mean?"

"It's pretty simple, actually," Mr. Monagan said. "It means that, yeah, there's dignity in risk. There's *dignity*—meaning feeling strong and good about yourself—in trying something that might seem hard for you to do."

"*Machismohhhhhhh, hombres!*" Peewee said, laughing.

"Well, not quite, Peewee," Mr. Monagan said. "I just mean that, at the end of the day, this is the *Kids* of Widney Junior High. It's *your* band, guys. I'm only your teacher. *You're* the band. *You're* the Kids."

"Okkaaaaay . . . ," Tanesa said. "We're listening."

"Well, if I took care of a band problem *for* you, where's the risk there for you all? Where's the dignity there for you? You're all getting older. I've known some of you for almost five years now. I've seen you get more mature—"

"Even me, Michael?" Peewee asked, belching loudly, with a Cheshire Cat grin. The other Kids laughed, and I couldn't help myself either.

"Even you, Peewee," Mr. Monagan answered, smiling brighter than ever. "I know you guys can handle this on your own. And part of that is what—"

"'Learned helplessness,' right?" Shelly said.

"Yeah, it's what 'learned helplessness' is about," Mr. Monagan said. "I know that, especially in a lot of special-ed programs, that can be an issue. Some of you and some of your classmates have had well-meaning teachers and aides in your classes. And they want to be nice and help you out as much as possible. But there's a point where if they help you out *too* much—tying your shoe for you, for example, even if you already know how to do it on your own—you'll end up giving into what is called 'learned helplessness.' You stop thinking you can do it on your own."

"I think we *allllll* know how to tie our shoes, Michael!" Tanesa said, bursting out in the loudest laughter yet.

"I like *double* knotting my shoelaces," Shelly proclaimed. "Double, double knots. Knots, knots, knots!"

"Well, that's good, Shelly," Mr. Monagan said. "But if someone else kept doing it for you all the time, you might stop doing it yourself, and that's not good. You're becoming an adult in the upcoming years, and the best way I can really teach you guys, be a true band leader for you here, a true *teacher*, is by giving you the ability to have that dignity of risk without giving into learned helplessness."

There was a pause. Mr. Monagan looked at me and winked.

I tried to wink back but couldn't. (I was working on my wink at the time. I couldn't keep from doing it with both eyes. It would end up being less a wink and more a *blink*.)

Peewee leapt for his big green jacket on the floor by my feet and zipped up like a superhero costuming up for a battle. "Awwww, Michael's right, *muchachos!* This is our band, and it's our job to get Cain back. Thanks, Michael!"

"Always happy to be of help," Mr. Monagan said.

And with that, the rest of the band got ready to leave, with Shelly calling his mom to pick everyone up and take them (and me!) to Cain's family's grocery store.

We had tried to get Cain back a few times already, but now it was time to get it done *right*.

Off we went to the store, not saying anything in Shelly's mom's minivan on the way there. She even asked at one point why we were all so serious. Daniel replied that we had a lot on our minds. Peewee said we were on a mission.

And we were ready to accomplish our mission at last!

Into Cain's grocery store we went ... ready to lay down the law and tell Cain he had to come back into the band, that we'd do whatever we had to to get him the money to give to his family to make up for his not being there after school ...

... until Peewee tripped on his way in on the gray welcome mat and knocked over a shelf of canned pickled jalapenos ... which knocked over a shelf of cans of black beans ... which knocked over ...

Welllllllllll, you get the point. Unfortunately.

The entire store became one gargantuan game of dominoes. Only it wasn't a *fun* game.

"PEEWEEEEEEEEEEEE!!!" Cain screamed.

Whoops.

Mission: *non*-accomplished.

CHAPTER 14

All About Love and Stuff

"Hmmmm . . . ," I said as I was walking with Peewee next to me on the sidewalk early that evening.

"Yeeaaaahhh," Peewee said, head down and watching his shoes as he trudged along, shamefaced.

"That was pretty crazy earlier," I said.

"Oh, yeah, it was, *muchacho*," Peewee said. "Total *nonsense*."

We didn't say anything for a few moments before I added:

"Geez, the whole grocery store."

"The whole thing, *muchacho*," Peewee said.

"Guess there's no way Cain's going to be able to rejoin the band after that snafu, huh?"

"Oh, heck, yeah. No way," Peewee said, still looking down at the ground as we kept walking. "Cain posted on his Instagram that he'll be off even from *school* for the next two weeks to help his whole family clean up."

"Are you gonna take off any days too to help?"

"Naaaaahhh," Peewee said. "I have enough absences already. If I get any more, Widney'll give me the boot! And we can't have that."

We kept walking.

"But, uh, you're gonna help Cain's family, right?"

"Heck, yeah!" Peewee said loudly, looking at me now and stopping short. I stopped too to really see his face and how sorry he was when he said, "After we're done with the concert tomorrow, I'll be working at Cain's bodega this weekend and next weekend to help out. I just wish that we had made some money with our businesses earlier this week so we could get Cain off the hook long enough to play the Key Club show with us."

I was about to start walking again when Peewee started going up the lawn toward the house before us. "Come on, *hombre!*"

I turned back to Peewee to see he was walking to a small, pinkish house with bars on the windows and a large gate on the front door.

"Wait, who lives here?" I asked.

"Who do you think?" Peewee answered. "This is where Elisa lives!"

I ran up to Peewee, whispering in case she was close to the door or something. "Elisa? But she's so angry with you right now!"

"I *know, muchacho,*" Peewee said, whispering back. "But since I screwed up everything with Cain, the least I can do is finally be a real man here and tell Elisa how I feel and that I really am sorry. If I can't help get Cain back in the

104

band, I can at least get Elisa to not be so upset when we're at the show tomorrow night. We can't have her being all ticked off on the other side of the stage. No Cain? That's bad, *dude*. But an angry *Bomba* on the stage? That's *really* bad, you know? It could ruin the whole concert, no?"

"Is that the only reason we're here?"

Peewee smiled and shook his head. He knew exactly what I was saying. "Awwww ... What can I say? I really like her, Robbie. I miss her, you know, bro?"

I didn't really know what he meant, to be honest. I had never had a girlfriend before. Frankly, I thought we were all a little young for that, but who was I to judge?

Although, sure, when I went to a sleepover camp for a long Memorial Day weekend last year, there was a girl I partnered with one of the nights when we were doing a square dance thing, and we ended up hanging out the next day at lunch too. That was pretty cool. It felt really good ... especially in my stomach.

I guess Peewee missed that good stomach feeling?

"Well, then?" I asked.

Peewee pursed his lips, nodded, wiped his forehead of some sweat droplets, and rang the bell next to the black gated door that kind of made me think of a cage some people put loud dogs in when they're barking too much.

We waited. I put my hand on Peewee's shoulder. He turned to me and beamed brightly.

The door opened. It was Elisa's dad. "Ayyyy, Peewee, how ya doin', buddy?"

"Awww, you know, same ol' same ol'."

We all stood there for a few seconds before Elisa's dad seemed to finally notice I was there, too. "Ayyyy, and you're ... Ryan?"

"Robbie," I said. "I'm new to Widney."

"You're in the band now too, right?"

"Not ... exactly," I said, not sure how to put it. "I'm more of, like ... uhhh ..."

"A groupie!" Elisa's dad sputtered out, with a huge grin on his face.

"Aww, Robbie's one of our assistant managers, buddy," Peewee said, putting *his* hand on *my* shoulder now. He turned to me and winked. I swear, I tried to wink back, but it still just came out a blink.

I blushed, but then Elisa's dad opened up the gate around the door and let us in.

"You guys probably want to see Elisa, eh? Have a feeling you're not here only to say hi to *me*."

"Ohh, if she's around, that'd be great," Peewee said. "She's not doing homework or nothing, is she? Taking a nap?"

"No, no, no," Elisa's dad said. "She's up in her room reading. She got some really good news today. I'm sure she'll be happy to see you both."

"Thank you!" Peewee said, delighted.

As we walked past Elisa's dad, he pulled Peewee back for a moment. "I think she'll be ... *really* happy to see *you*." He nodded, and Peewee nodded back. "I know she's given you a little bit of a hard time lately, Peewee."

"Aww, well, truthfully, buddy, I think I deserved it," Peewee said.

"Don't I know it!" Elisa's dad said, patting Peewee on the back. "If you guys want anything to eat, I can bring up some snacks. Elisa knows what we've got in the kitchen."

"What's the good news?" I asked.

"Oh, I'll let Elisa tell you," Elisa's dad said before walking toward the living room and plopping down on his chair across from where the TV was blaring a soccer game.

Up the brown shag-carpet stairs we walked, and I could feel Peewee placing his hand on my shoulder again on the way. It made me feel good to know I could be here with him as moral support.

It was becoming clearer to me now that we were becoming true friends; that I really *was* a member of the band—if only on the sidelines—and that they needed me as much as I needed them.

We got upstairs. I let Peewee lead the way, since I hadn't been here before. Then we stepped down the dark, narrow hallway with cream-colored walls. Walls crowded by pictures of Elisa and her dad together in different places like Disneyland and Knott's Berry Farm and Magic Mountain and the beach.

Once we arrived at Elisa's door (with one of those personalized fake license plates on it that had her name affixed to it), Peewee stopped. He breathed deep.

"You okay, Peewee?" I whispered.

"Just my stomach, *muchacho*," Peewee said. "It's doing backflips and front flips and sideways flips too."

"Here, take my hand," I said to Peewee. "Close your eyes. And take some deep breaths with me, all right?"

We did just that, and I could feel Peewee's tight, sweaty grip on my hand. He was trembling. We were breathing together, in and out, slow and deep. It felt good. I hoped it helped Peewee too.

"Dad?" we heard from inside Elisa's room. Then the door opened.

The bright white light exploded through the doorway, and there was Elisa standing in her blue Kids of Widney Junior High shirt and large jean shorts. "Oh. Hello."

Peewee's eyes bolted open. He didn't say anything.

"Hey, Elisa, it's good to see you," I said.

She seemed nervous. "Uh . . . youuuuuu too . . . Robbie."

It was as though we were waiting for Peewee to say something. He didn't.

But . . .

. . . then he did.

"*Bomba*, you know you're my favorite person," Peewee said. I could see Elisa's eyes watering. "I'm sorry if I've said some things or done some things that made you feel less than that."

Elisa smiled bright, wiped her eyes, and lunged at Peewee.

Nuzzling her face into his chest, she gave him a tremendous bear hug . . . and in fact lifted him. I realized how incredibly strong Elisa is. There Peewee went, up and off the ground, his dirty blue sneakers dangling under him.

"Now *that's* what I call an uplifting moment!" I said. And we all laughed.

Minutes later, we were in Elisa's room together, sitting with our legs crossed on the stained, beige carpet by her bed. Peewee asked what the good news was that her dad had hinted at.

"Oh, man! I wanted it to be a surprise!" Elisa said, grinning. But then she couldn't help herself. She got up and went to her cluttered desk, grabbed a large white envelope, and came back to the floor with us.

"What is it, *gruñir*?" Peewee asked.

"I won!"

"What'd you win?" I asked.

"The big prize!"

"What big prize, *gruñir*?" Peewee asked.

"The *biggest* prize! I won it all!"

"But ... *what did you WIN*?" Peewee and I both asked. Then we looked at each other and laughed.

"My autobiography won first prize in the Young Writers Contest," Elisa said, ecstatic. "Even though it's still a work in progress, they accepted it, and the judges decided my book was the best ... and an excerpt of it will be in the *Young Writers Literary Journal* ... and I got $5,000!"

"$5,000?!" Peewee and I both said together. This time, we *didn't* laugh. (We're talking $5,000 here, folks. Nothing funny about *that!*)

"What are you going to do with $5,000, *Bomba?*" Peewee asked.

"What do you think I'm gonna do with it? I'm going over to Cain's grocery store to give it to him. This way, he can pay his family, so they can hire someone else to do what he's been doing after school, and come back to the band! Kids of Widney Junior High forever!"

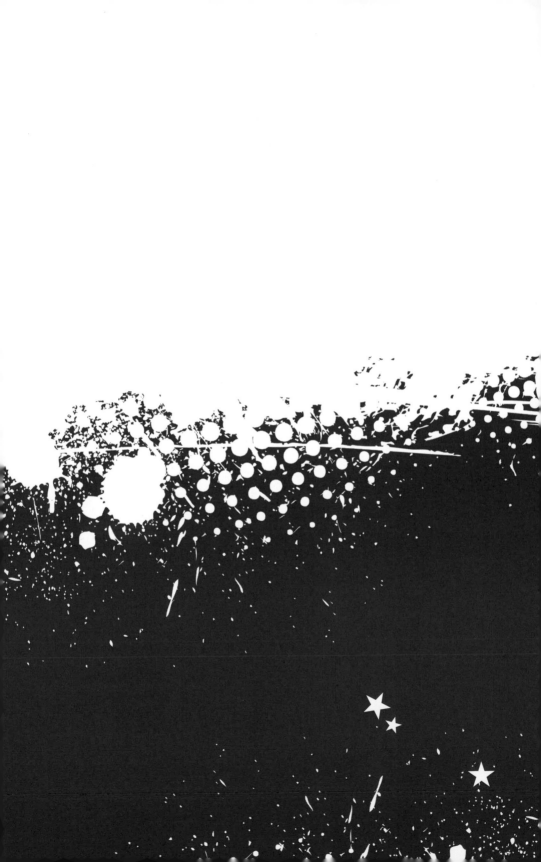

CHAPTER 15

Come On, Cain!

The next day. Friday. Three hours till showtime.

Three hours until the Key Club performance. The show that could change everyone's lives. The show that hopefully would lead to the Kids of Widncy Junior High getting signed by a big record label.

And where were we?

Outside Cain's family's grocery store, of course. Everyone was there: the whole band, including Mr. Monagan with his guitar strapped to his back.

We all looked at one another, realizing this was the last chance we had to get Cain back onboard—at least for this one show—hoping beyond hope that Elisa's prize money would be the deciding factor in Cain coming with us.

"Okay, gang, let's do it," Mr. Monagan said. "Remember: it's up to all of *you*. You can do it."

"Let's go!" Shelly called out.

"Yeah, everybody!" Tanesa agreed. "Move it, Kids of Widney Junior High!"

In we went, and there was Cain, sweeping the floor and helping his family continue to clean up some of the leftover mess that Peewee had made just two days earlier.

"*Hola, ¿qué tal?*," Cain looked up to say in our direction.

"Cain, *tus amigos en la banda están aquí*," Cain's aunt said, stepping away, and taking the other family members working around him to the backroom so we could all chat.

Cain stopped sweeping and stopped smiling. "I . . . thought I told you *no*. No, I'm . . . I'm n-n-n-not coming back to the band. No."

"But Cain . . . we really need you," Tanesa said.

"No."

"But Cain, if you don't sing 'Respect,' we might not impress the record label exec enough to sign us," Daniel said.

"But Cain, you're one of the main reasons people come to see us at all, *muchacho!*" Peewee said.

"No."

"But Cain . . . what about *this?*" Elisa said, holding up her large white envelope filled with the $5,000 she'd won.

Cain did not say "no" this time. Instead, he started sniffing. *SNIFF SNIFF SNIFF.*

"$5,000?!" he said, dropping his broom and jumping up and down happily. "Just for *me*, Elisa?"

"Well, for your family, Cain," Elisa said. "Because this will also be for the band. I know you have your loyalty to the store. But with this money, your family can hire another worker to come in and fill in for you while you play with us tonight and hopefully from here on in. Especially if we get signed by the label!"

"Oh, my goodness, Elisa!" Cain said, smiling brighter than I'd ever seen him, jumping up and down over and over again. (Normally Cain reminds me of Winnie the Pooh, but right then, he was *totally* being Tigger!)

"Wait a second, Cain," I said. "You can *smell* $5,000?"

"Ohhh, yeahhhhhhhh, Robbie, my good friend," Cain said. "Like . . . like $5,000, no?"

I looked to Peewee and he shrugged his shoulders. Everyone has his or her special talents, I guess!

"I can also smell th-th-th-that Peewee ate another egg-egg-egg salad sandwich at lunch today," Cain said.

"Naaaahhh," Tanesa corrected. "He had *ten!*"

Everybody laughed, and then Mr. Monagan piped in. "So, Cain, does this mean you're back in the band, then?"

"Oh, yesssss, Mr. Monagan, yes!" Cain said. "Yes, I dooooooooo!"

"*Tú todo bien ahí fuera, Cain?*" we could all hear Cain's aunt in the backroom behind the dirty plastic sheet call out to him.

Cain's smile dropped.

He called to his aunt: "*Sí, tía.*" He stopped jumping up and down. He reached for his broom but had some trouble finding it on the floor. Daniel used his cane to guide him, shuffling up away from the rest of the band to grab the broom and hand it to Cain, who started sweeping again.

"Cain?" Elisa asked.

"I'm s-s-s-sorry, Elisa," Cain said. "But it's not j-j-j-j-just about the money, okay? I have to help out my f-f-f-family. Thank you, b-b-b-but—"

And that's when Daniel stopped Cain from sweeping by placing a gentle hand on his chest. "Look, Cain. I know you have your family to think about here, along with their store. You know that . . . I . . . I have had in the past my doubts about the band too. But you know what? The reason I really want to do this, and why I keep doing it, and why I think we *all* need to keep being the Kids of Widney Junior High, is because . . . is because we make people happy."

"Happy?" Cain said, looking up to Daniel before him.

"Yeah, Cain," Tanesa said, stepping toward Daniel and him. "Why else you think we be doin' this? We all wanna be makin' ourselves and everyone coming to our shows happy, right?"

"Especially these days, Cain," Elisa said. "It's so important to do whatever we can . . . to make people happy. There's so many people so scared and angry out there. If they can come to our shows and feel good for even an hour or two, that's a big deal. Isn't it?"

No one said anything for a few seconds . . . but I could see that Cain was contemplating what everyone was getting at. Right there and then, like some kind of magical sign from the universe, we heard it on the radio:

"For all those fans of the Kids of Widney Junior High out there, all you folks heading to the live show at the Key Club on Sunset Blvd., we have for you now our favorite song and maybe yours, too: 'Respect'!"

BOOM.

The Kids of Widney Junior High on the radio. And it was 'Respect.' Cain's song. *Thee* song.

It began, and Cain started tapping his foot to the beat. The other band members began tapping too, bopping their heads. Mr. Monagan smiled wide. He was so proud, watching his students groove to their very own music. I was proud too.

Cain began belting out his lyrics, and before I knew it, we had our own private Kids of Widney Junior High concert happening right before my eyes, there in Cain's family's grocery store.

Once the song was over, the Kids gave each other high-fives and cheered. I got into it too, giving hugs to everyone and shaking hands and the whole shebang. It was probably the best Kids of Widney Junior High rehearsal (if you wanna call it that) that I'd ever seen. And I couldn't *wait* to see them at the Key Club that night.

"You coming with us, Cain?" Daniel asked.

"Oh, yeah, Daniel, my very good friend," Cain said. "B-b-b-but j-j-just one thing . . ."

"What's that, *bro?*" Peewee asked.

"We b-b-b-b-b-better better get g-g-g-going!" Cain said, excitedly. "Otherwise we'll be late to our own show!"

CHAPTER 16

Life in the Too-Fast Lane

Have you ever been pulled over by the police?

I have. Or, I guess I should say, I've been in the car when someone has. I never thought it was something I'd experience—my mom is usually (repeat: *usually*) a pretty good driver. But that early evening, on our way to the Key Club, we *did* get pulled over.

I guess there were a whole *lot* of things that I never thought would happen to me until I met the Kids of Widney Junior High. Here I was again, on yet another crazy adventure. (Or what some might call a *mis*adventure?)

Whatever you want to call it, there I was in the middle between Elisa and Peewee (who were holding hands over my lap), and Daniel up in the passenger seat next to Elisa's dad, who had been driving.

I say *had* been driving because, of course, we were now stopped and waiting for the police officer who'd pulled us

over to come and tell Elisa's dad that we were in some serious trouble.

Mr. Monagan was behind us, and I could see in the rearview mirror that he was pulling over to wait for us with Cain and Shelly in his car.

What had happened was we had all been in such a rush to the Key Club show that we had stopped paying attention to the speed limit, and, well, when you break the law, trouble abounds.

This time, we're not talking about the kind of trouble Peewee was used to getting into (or, for that matter, getting *us* into!). We're talking sirens, blinking red-and-blue lights, and what they call in some of the movies Tanesa would show me at her house, "the fuzz."

"Oh, man, I was *worried* we were going too fast!" Daniel said from the passenger seat, shuddering. He was scared. We all were.

"We'll be all right, buddy," Elisa's dad said calmly. He seemed oddly used to this sort of thing.

"Don't worry," Elisa leaned over to whisper to me, her hand still holding Peewee's over my lap. "My dad is used to this sort of thing."

Oh, geez!

"Maybe we'll get to be on an episode of *Cops!*" Peewee said. "That's my favorite show."

"I certainly hope not, Peewee," Daniel said. "I don't want this to ruin the reputation of the Kids of Widney Junior High. Or mine either. This better not stand in the way of my going to Columbia!" (Daniel dreamed of going to

Columbia University in New York City to study broadcast journalism, I should add here.)

"You're just in the passenger seat, *bro!*" Peewee called back to Daniel.

Elisa squeezed Peewee's hand so tight, I could feel the gripping over my lap. "Come on now, Luis," Elisa said. "We're all in this together. Let's just stay calm and . . . and let my dad handle it. Like he always does."

"Like he *always* does?" I asked, with no response from anyone else in the car. *Oh, geeeeeeez!*

There was a knock at the window.

Behind the knocking fist was the largest policeman I've ever seen in my life. (True, I've only seen maybe three or four. But you get the point.)

Elisa's dad lowered the window. "Can I help you, buddy?"

"Do you have any idea how fast you were going, sir?"

Now I could feel that *Peewee's* hand was growing tighter around *Elisa's* hand.

I was meanwhile sweating bullets, and I could see Daniel was wiping his brow of sweat too. I'm telling you, compared to watching scary movies at Tanesa's house, this was a whole new level of fear!

Oh geez oh geez oh geez oh geeeeeeez!

"I'd say maybe 70, 75," Elisa's dad said, as calm as ever.

"You were going 77 in a 65, sir."

"Will have to get my speedometer checked, huh, buddy?" Elisa's dad said, smiling politely.

"Ooooooohhhh!" Peewee whispered. I think he was actually *enjoying* this! I guess once a troublemaker, always a troublemaker . . .

"Antonio, please," Elisa whispered back to him.

"Sir, may I ask what the rush was all about, then?"

"We have to get these kids to their concert at the Key Club in less than twenty minutes, buddy," Elisa's dad said.

"Concert?" the police officer scoffed in disbelief. "What, are these guys in a band or something?"

"Ya darn tootin' they are!" Elisa's dad said, smiling brighter.

"Your band have a name?"

"We're the Kids of Widney Junior High, sir," Daniel chimed in, trembling so much you could hear his teeth clattering while he said it.

The humongous police officer paused. His eyebrows furrowed and he stepped backward. "Wait a second . . . *You're* the Kids of Widney Junior High?"

"Yes, sir!" Peewee cried out triumphantly. "We sure are!"

"Oh, my goodness!" the police officer said, slapping his leg and breaking out in a grin that was nearly bigger than he was. "You're my favorite rock band!"

"What?!" I couldn't help but cry out. "Are you serious?"

"Indubitably, young man!" the policeman said. "We listen to 'Let's Get Busy' and 'Life Without the Cow' all the time at the station. *All* the officers at our station listen to you guys."

"Isn't that something?" Elisa's dad said, winking at me in the rearview mirror. I tried winking back at him . . . and *did it!* I finally winked! Sometimes, I suppose, you do your best work under pressure.

"You know, I have a daughter who has special needs, too," the policeman said. "She's not old enough to go to school yet, but when she is, I really hope we'll be able to send her to Widney Junior High so she can maybe one day be part of your band . . ."

"We hope so too, officer," Daniel said, no longer shaking. "We'll save a place for her. Everyone is always welcome to join the Kids to express themselves creatively."

"I really appreciate that," the officer said. "And you must be . . . Daniel? Is that right?"

"It is!" Daniel said, clapping his hands happily. "And this here is Peewee, Elisa, Elisa's dad, and our assistant manager, Robbie."

"Pleased to meet all of you," the officer said.

Wow. *Assistant manager*, Daniel had confirmed. It really was true. I was the Kids' assistant manager. It wasn't just something Peewee had been kidding around about when I first met Elisa's dad the other day. They really, *really* meant it!

"I hate to break up the gabfest here, sir . . ." Peewee began. "But, uh . . . we *do* have a show to get to, sir, and, wellll—"

"Oh, my good golly gravy, yes," the officer said, getting serious once more and stealing my catchphrase. "I know all about your big show tonight. The guys and gals at the station are looking forward to listening to the live stream of it on the Key Club website. Now that I think of it, I was hoping to get back there in time to listen too!"

"When's your shift end?" Elisa's dad asked.

Checking his watch, the officer answered, "Oh, geez, technically I'm off-duty right after this!"

"Why don't you come with us to the show as a special guest?" Daniel asked. "If you want to call your wife, you're more than welcome to bring her and your daughter too. Free of charge!"

"Are you kidding me? That would be incredible! I'll call them on the way!" the officer said, jumping up and down like Cain when he's excited. "And to make sure you get there on time, I'll give you an official police escort! Follow me!"

We all cheered and gave each other high-fives. Elisa's dad texted Mr. Monagan and told him what was going on, and off we went following our new friend the police officer, who blared his siren and turned on his red-and-blue lights, but this time to *help* us get there faster *and* safer!

Key Club, here we come!

CHAPTER 17

The Really Big Show!

There I was.

At the Key Club. *Thee* Key Club.

On Sunset Boulevard.

For a kid who had just moved to the area, being in Hollywood, California, at all was already a big deal. And now here I was at a big-deal rock club on the famous "strip," as they call it. (I'm still trying to figure out who "they" is, but right now, it simply doesn't matter!)

I'm watching my very favorite rock band, the Kids of Widney Junior High. And they are . . . *KILLING IT!*

I knew the KOWJH were a sight to behold. I knew they had the goods. I knew they were the real deal. From the moment I first met them, from the moment I first heard them rehearse in Mr. Monagan's garage. Here we were a few months later, and I was getting to witness them bring it to the stage at the club and really show everyone *else* what their music was all about.

About good times. About laughter and fun. About embracing what it is that's different and "weird" about yourself. About feeling confident in who you are as an individual. About cracking jokes. Supporting one another as friends. Making sure everyone has a chance to express themselves how they see fit. Remembering not to feel bad for yourself when things get rough, but rather to build yourself up and overcome whatever obstacle comes your way.

That really is what the Kids are all about and what their music is all about.

Watching them from the audience (and, boy, was it *packed!*)—there in the dark club with the spotlights on the Kids on stage, dancing and singing, Peewee and Elisa holding hands again like they used to, the band members all together sweating, bopping up and down, giving each other hugs and high-fives, smiling at one another and making jokes between the songs—I knew that this was going to be a night I'd never, ever forget.

The audience around me—all different ages, all different kinds of people, all wearing different kinds of clothes, with different kinds of haircuts (and hair colors! pink and purple, some of them!), all different heights and sizes and ages— they were sweating and laughing and holding each other up and bopping up and down too.

I may not have known most of the other people around me (there were plenty of fellow students from Widney and a couple of folks I'd seen come by rehearsal a few times, and of course the Kids' family members were there). But I still felt strongly that these were *all* my friends. Friends bonded together through our love of the band, the music, and the individual Kids of Widney Junior High members themselves.

You know something *really* cool? Guess who else I spotted in the crowd? Remember those original bullies who nearly knocked my clock out my first day at school when I first met Peewee and got into this whole crazy adventure to begin with? The ones who looked like ogres? They were there in the back, dancing and jumping up and down wildly to the music too.

The particularly large fellow who didn't seem to know how to wipe his mouth of chocolate (and still had some over his lip, I could see!) turned to me through the crowd. He saw that I saw him, he nodded and smiled, I smiled back, and we both went right on dancing to the music.

It was already a magical evening, and the show had only begun a few minutes earlier. *I've never felt more at home in my entire life.*

The Kids finished up "Throw Away the Trash," and the audience went hog wild.

The roar of the collective cheering gave me tingling sensations all over in the best possible way. Especially since I was raising my arms and cheering along with everyone else! I may not be into sports, but now I understood why people love going to games and cheering along with the crowds for their favorite teams and players.

Shelly came up to the front of the stage, catching his breath from the last song, wiped his head of sweat, and with a humongous grin on his face hollered into the microphone in his hand, "WE ARE . . . *THE KIDS OF WIDNEY JUNIOR HIGH!!*"

The audience completely lost their minds. We had transmogrified into a pit of sweaty, wild, smiley friends cheering louder than anything I could imagine. It was great. And it was about to get even greater . . .

"From the band, all up here on stage, to *you* out in the audience," Shelly said, pointing to all of us, "we want to make a very special dedication to the man who came all the way here to see us from the one and only Wyld Style Records, Mister . . . Frank . . . Tomlinson!"

Everyone cheered once again, and we all turned to where Shelly was specifically pointing now.

Indeed, there, toward the back of the room, was a guy who looked *exactly* like you'd expect a big-deal record exec to look like—long black hair, big glasses, a goatee, a rad black leather jacket from the eighties . . . and one other thing maybe you might not have expected: he was sitting . . . in a wheelchair.

He gave Shelly an enthusiastic thumbs-up and was clearly enjoying the show as much as everyone else. We all clapped and shouted our lungs out.

"For our new friend Frank from Wyld Style Records, we just want to say *ONE . . . THING*: we hope you'll *respect* our next song. Because this one's for *you*, Frank!"

YEAH!

Shelly handed over the mike to Cain, who came shuffling up to the front of the stage. The Kids went right into their rendition of "Respect," with Cain on lead vocals. And boy, if I thought Cain was typically a happy little guy in the past, now I *really* saw what it meant when Cain got excited!

He was absolutely incredible through the whole song, and the band backed him up like he hadn't missed a single rehearsal. The band and he gelled so well I *knew* that if this was the record producer's favorite song, he wasn't being let down tonight.

I *knew* the Kids were about to get their record deal.

But there were still more announcements first!

Once "Respect" was over, Cain screamed out happily to everyone in the crowd, "Thank you very much! We're the Kids of Widney Junior High, and we're b-b-b-best friends! Thank you! Thank you! Thhhhhhhank you v-v-v-v-very much!"

But that wasn't the kicker . . .

"I have something I w-w-w-want to s-s-s-say!" Cain shouted out to the crowd gleefully. "It's really important, guys! Yeah!"

We all quieted down to hear what Cain was about to say next:

"I just want to say . . . I just want to say that tonight was v-v-v-very special to me. And that I'm not gonna stop, no! I just want to say that I'm gonna come back to the band p-p-p-p-permanently again!"

YESSSSSSSS!

The crowd got even louder than before, cheering and applauding, screaming and laughing all together as one big solid unit of people enjoying their favorite rock band.

Cain back in the band for good? This was the best news he could have announced.

"I'm still gonna help out my *tío* at our family's grocery store on weekends. But with the help of my friend Elisa here, we can afford to hire someone to w-w-w-ork on weekday nights so I can … keep rehearsing with the bands! Oh, yeah! I'm a rock star grocery cl-cl-clerk!"

The Kids then went right from the announcement to their next song, "Act Your Age." One of my all-time favorites!

As soon as the song was over, Tanesa stepped up to the front to have her own announcement now, and this one would be the one I would *really* never forget. *What did she have to say?*

"All of us here with the band, ya know, we havin' a good time and all, and we all so glad you all is, too," Tanesa started. "But there's one person we really want to thank for all his help and his support, and that's our good new friend Robbie. Where you at now, Robbie? Raise yo hand!"

Everyone in the crowd turned to where Tanesa was looking and pointing (at me!), and I simply didn't know what to do or say. The whole place was silent. It was as though they were waiting for me to do something. And then, you know what?—I did: I raised my hand up high and shouted, "We are *all* the Kids of Widney Junior High!"

I don't think anyone in the crowd or on stage stopped screaming and jumping up and down, cheering for at least five minutes. People were hugging me and giving me high-fives, and I could see all the Kids of Widney Junior High up there smiling at me, and Mr. Monagan giving me his own thumbs-up, winking.

I winked back, just as excited that now I knew how!

FINAL CHAPTER

The End Is Only the Beginning

So, that's my story about how I first met and became friends with *thee* Kids of Widney Junior High.

Heck, it's the story of how I became a *part* of the Kids of Widney Junior High.

Like pretty much every other story, things didn't always go the way I'd have wanted. There were some tough times in there, for sure. Hard decisions we all had to make. Things we had to figure out that I wasn't sure about. But in the end, I'm glad things worked out as they did, and I'm glad I ended up where I am right now.

Just as the Kids always had (and, as I'd learn, always *would*), we never saw ourselves as victims of circumstances. Instead, we worked hard to figure out how to take control of those circumstances to the best of our abilities, and we did it *together* as a team. As a band.

Sure, we may not be able to control the waves, but we *can* always control the way we decide to surf. And that's the final lesson of my friendship with the Kids of Widney Junior High.

* * *

At home, in my bed. The morning after the Kids of Widney Junior High show. Looking up at my ceiling. It kind of looks like cottage cheese up there. Sometimes I like trying to count as many of the cottage cheese bumps as I can.

But right now, I'm not counting anything. I'm reaching over to the new, beautiful guitar my mom got me, which I found wrapped in a red bow after Elisa's dad dropped me off after the concert last night.

I'm picking up the guitar, taking off the bow, and—still lying on my back—starting to play around with the strings, starting to make some noise. Not necessarily *music*, mind you. But noise. I guess you could call it "musical noise," sure. (It sounds a little like one of my *other* favorite rock bands, Sonic Youth, but I still have a long way to go before I get *there!*)

I know if I keep playing around on this thing, if I keep up my practice like I do with my meditation and like the Kids of Widney Junior High do with their own rehearsals, that maybe one day I can make my own songs and music too.

If the Kids of Widney Junior High can do it, why can't I? All I need to do is believe in myself like they do, and put in the time, effort, and *practice*.

I know the Kids made a big impression on the record executive last night, and I know there will be plenty more stories about their continued rise to fame to tell you in the future to come.

I can't wait to see what happens next, but for now, excuse me while I attempt a few tunes on my new ax . . .

A moment with PEEWEE

Although our own Kids of Widney Junior High member Peewee is a fictional character, we are grateful to real-life Kids of Widney High member Peewee for allowing us to be loosely inspired by him in the creation of said book character. The actual Peewee is forty years old, attended Joseph P. Widney High School for the majority of his primary schooling, lives with autism, and has been a part of the Kids of Widney High for more than two decades. A favorite song of his to sing is, not surprisingly, the rousing punk rock tribute "I Make My Teachers Mad." Peewee enjoys working on computers, watching Steven Seagal movies, and spending time with his longtime girlfriend, fellow former Widney High student and Kids member Elisa.

The following is a transcript of a recorded conversation between Peewee and author Mathew Klickstein from April 2019 that was conducted specifically for this book.

MK: When did you get involved with the Kids of Widney High?

PW: '99.

MK: Why did you decide to join the band?

PW: It was cool, because it gave us a chance to practice music and singing. My favorite band at the time was Stone Temple Pilots, and I wanted to do something similar to them.

MK: Had you been a fan of the Kids before you joined?

PW: No, I hadn't really heard of them until Elisa told me about the band. So, I went and talked with Mike [Monagan], and he thought it would be a cool idea for me to become part of the group.

MK: What is your favorite part about being in the band?

PW: Traveling to different places to perform, singing in front of different kinds of people. It gives them a chance to know and hear that we're out there too. That there are people with special abilities out there making music like other bands.

MK: Why is that important to you?

PW: Because it's important for these people listening to us and coming to our shows to know that we're not only what some may call "handicapped." That we're more than that. We can do things some people may not think we can do, like make and sing our own music. For me, it's also important that we could introduce something different out there. A different point of view that other bands may not have.

MK: The Kids have enjoyed a lot of support, especially early on, from other more established bands like No Doubt, the Beastie Boys, Marilyn Manson, Nirvana, Jackson Browne, Osaka Popstar, and Mike Patton. Did you find this to be helpful?

PW: Oh, yeah. Bands would let us open for them, or they'd express their love for our music in interviews, and that was a big part of what helped us get going in the earlier days. And then, of course, there was *The Ringer*, the movie we were in, which got the word out about the Kids of Widney High in an even-bigger way too. We noticed people recognized us more and came to more of our shows after *The Ringer*.

MK: What was that experience like? Being in a major motion picture?

PW: The people making *The Ringer* were awesome. They could have used other people to pretend to be us, but instead they preferred to have the actual group in the film.

MK: This is something you've talked with me about in the past, and I think is a good point: Why do you think it's important to have people with disabilities playing these parts in films and on TV instead of the typical case in which actors without disabilities tend to play these parts?

PW: Just like with our music, we want to be able to show *we can do this too*. In their mind, a lot of people think of us, again, as only being "retarded" and that we might not be able to act in films or on TV. I don't care if you put this in the interview and use that word, because I really do feel in their mind, yes, when a lot of people look at us, they see us as "retarded" kids or adults and that's it. If we play our music in front of them or they hear our albums or see us acting in movies and on TV, maybe we can show them otherwise. I don't really have the words for what I want to say, but I want people to know *we can perform!*

MK: You seemed reluctant to use the word "retarded" in your previous response. Is this a word that you find demeaning or hurtful?

PW: It's when people only see us that way that I get upset. You know something? Some day the people who maybe use that word a lot or who see us that way will have a family member that might end up in *our* alleyway, and that's when maybe they'll need to hear our song "Respect," right?! [*laughs*] Look, I've grown up my whole life with people using that word around me; I'm *not* hurt by it. I'm just trying to make a point: we're *more* than that word. I also want to say that not all of us feel this way. Some of us *are* hurt by that word, so I guess the other point is to be aware of when and how and who you use that word around, maybe. I don't speak for *everyone* who has a disability. These are only *my* personal feelings.

MK: It's a tough word, for sure, especially because its meaning has changed a lot over the years. Does that matter to you?

PW: Maybe the meaning of the word has changed over the years, but people inside haven't changed, I don't think. Which is why I'm glad this book is going out there, because this can be a good opportunity to emphasize what we're feeling and thinking about these kinds of things.

MK: Would you rather people not use that word at all, then?

PW: I do think people shouldn't use that word anymore. Most of the people with special needs I know don't like it.

MK: If it were up to you, how would persons outside of your community talk about and treat you?

PW: Like everyone else. Like anyone else they'd talk about or meet up with. Because we *all* have something going on that makes us different. There's no such thing as "normal."

MK: Daniel and I have had the discussion about how he doesn't necessarily like the idea of a "disabled community" at all, that you're all individuals and shouldn't be lumped in together in that way. What are your thoughts on this?

PW: We *are* all individuals with our own personalities. That's true. But we also don't want people to look at us a certain way and put us on the back burner because of our disabilities.

MK: If you could speak directly to the reader of this book right now, what would you tell this person?

PW: We are all different, but we're also very much the same. We all have our individual personalities, but we're also all human beings. Together. I'd say if you have any questions about any of these things, ask. When you're doing that, though, I think it's best to bring these things up *slowly* and maybe first try to make a friendship. Then, as time comes, you can bring it up eventually. You don't want to just whip it out right away, or we might feel you're making fun of us or something. Get to know the person, create a friendship, and then eventually, sure, you can bring it up and ask. It's about little steps at a time and respect. This is all a learning process, and everyone should just try the best they can.

MK: Last, what is it that you hope people will feel or think after they leave a Kids of Widney High show?

PW: That if they want to create their own music or band, not to be afraid. Don't let anything, even your disability, cloud your dreams. *Just go for it!*

About the guys who made this book

MATHEW KLICKSTEIN (author) is a longtime writer, filmmaker, and arts therapist who has written books on such topics as the early years of the Nickelodeon network, *The Simpsons*, and pop culture nostalgia itself. He's worked closely with the Kids of Widney High for more than two decades on numerous short films, music videos, and other creative projects. Mathew also produced and managed the Kids' sole headlining live tour, which he chronicled in the feature-length documentary *Act Your Age: The Kids of Widney High Story*. He lives with his wife, Becky, and their many books, albums, and tchotchkes. More on Mathew's ongoing shenanigans can be found at *www.MathewKlickstein.com*.

MICHAEL S. BRACCO (illustrator) has written and illustrated multiple science-fiction graphic novels over his career. These stories explore a wide array of social issues and relate to comic readers of all ages. His tales have delved into war-torn alien worlds in his NOVO series and literally brought the imaginations of young people to life in both wonderful and horribly monstrous ways in *The Creators*. He has also collaborated on multiple comic projects and is currently buried in his sketchbook surrounded by his wife, their daughter, and Bowie the Cat. For more on Michael's artwork and projects, check out *www.SpaghettiKiss.com*.

The creators of this book would like to offer our thanks to our publisher, Pete Schiffer, along with Tracee Groff, Kim Grandizio, Cheryl Weber, and Carey Massimini, who originally brought our proposal to the attention of the company, and everyone else at Schiffer Publishing for their faith in this unique project, their cheerful encouragement, and rock-hard support in helping us to put together a very special project about which we can all be immensely proud.

Special thanks are of course also owed to our continually supportive friends and family, the Kids of Widney High and Michael Monagan, and Petite Konstantin and the gang at L.A. GOAL.

If you're in need of assistance or would like to get involved, there are many resources to help and get you rockin' like the Kids of Widney Junior High

Abilities

https://www.abilities.com/

ADA (Americans with Disabilities Act) National Network

https://adata.org/

Amicus

https://www.amicusgroup.org/

The Arc

https://thearc.org/

ASAN (Autistic Self Advocacy Network)

https://autisticadvocacy.org/

Brain Injury Association of America

https://www.biausa.org/

CDK (Canines for Disabled Kids)

https://caninesforkids.org/

NMEDA (National Mobility Equipment Dealers Association)

https://nmeda.com/

Special Olympics

https://www.specialolympics.org/

U.S. Department of Health & Human Services

https://www.hhs.gov/

Volunteers of America

https://www.voa.org/people-with-disabilities

VSA (The Kennedy Center's International Organization on Arts and Disability)

https://www.kennedy-center.org/visit/accessibility/vsa/

Wheelchair Dancers Organization

https://www.wheelchairdancers.org/

Wounded Warrior Project

https://www.woundedwarriorproject.org/